THE GATE OF DAYS

THE GATE OF DAYS

THE BOOK OF TIME II

GUILLAUME PRÉVOST

Translated by
WILLIAM RODARMOR

ARTHUR A. LEVINE BOOKS

An Imprint of Scholastic Inc.

Library of Congress Cataloging-in-Publication Data

Prévost, Guillaume.
[Sept pièces. English]
The gate of days : the Book of Time II / by Guillaume Prévost ; translated by
William Rodarmor. — 1st ed.
p. cm.
Summary: While seeking the seven magical coins that will allow him to reach
his father, who is trapped in the castle of Vlad Tepes, Sam Faulkner travels to
such places as ancient Delphi, a Stone Age cave, and 1930s Chicago.
ISBN 978-0-439-88376-4 (hardcover : alk. paper) [1. Time travel — Fiction.
2. Missing persons — Fiction.] I. Rodarmor, William. II. Title.
PZ7.P9246Gat 2008
[Fic] — dc22
2007050263

ISBN-13: 978-0-439-88376-4
ISBN-10: 0-439-88376-8

10 9 8 7 6 5 4 3 2 1   08 09 10 11 12

Printed in the U.S.A.

First edition, October 2008

CONTENTS

CHAPTER ONE

Burglary

The inside of the dinosaur's stomach reeked of epoxy and paint. Sam Faulkner crouched all the way in the back of the space, just where the body narrowed to a long fiberglass tail, and he was ready to move — to get out of not just the huge Baryonyx where he'd been hiding all evening, but out of the Sainte-Mary Museum. As soon as the guards completed their rounds, he would slip over to the coin room, take what he needed — Sam preferred to think of it as borrowing — and return to the dinosaur until the museum reopened in the morning. Then he would rescue his father.

He had never *wanted* to spend his nights hiding in a dinosaur's butt, Sam thought wryly. Indeed, if someone had told him two weeks earlier that he was going to steal from the museum — or that he would travel to ancient Egypt or World War I, or that his father was stuck in the fifteenth century as a prisoner of Dracula — he never would have believed them. But once you knew time travel was possible, and that a squat little statue in your basement could send you hurtling into the past, all sorts of possibilities — even necessities — opened up as well.

He tensed at the sound of footsteps in the hall. Two night watchmen switched on the light and walked by, a couple of feet from him, talking.

"The Baryo there isn't finished either. Seems the painter won't come back till he's paid what he's owed."

"There's no more money for it," said the other man. "The curator says the city won't increase the subsidy. We need some new exhibits to bring people in. Did you read in the paper about that Greek thing they auctioned in London? The Navel of the World or some such? An old stone, and it went for ten million dollars in less than ten minutes! Our little museum can't afford that!"

"No kidding! Won't be long before they start firing people to cut costs!"

The guards were still grumbling as they crossed the hall to the far door and went out, leaving Sam alone again. He wolfed down two chocolate-nut bars he'd thought to buy from the vending machine and waited for the next round. The guards passed through again an hour and a quarter later, arguing about the merits of their favorite hockey teams. One was a staunch supporter of the Canadiens; the other swore by the Maple Leafs. Even though Sam felt that no one could match the Senators when they were on a roll, he was careful not to speak up. If the dinosaur suddenly gave its opinion on the Stanley Cup, the two men would surely have heart attacks.

Sam looked at his watch. It was past ten o'clock, and he had about fifty minutes to carry out his plan. In order to operate the stone statue that allowed him to time-travel, he needed a coin with a hole in it, one that could date from any period of history. Once the coin was set onto the sun carved in the center of the stone, the statue would shoot him through time to some period of its own mysterious choosing; there was no way to know where he might end up. But on one of his adventures, Sam had learned he might be able to choose his destination if he had *seven* of these magic coins. And as his father was in the clutches of Vlad Tepes — a bloody tyrant of medieval Romania, the man who had served as a model for Dracula — there wasn't a moment to be lost.

The problem was, Sam had only three coins. His cousin Lily had suggested that he try the Sainte-Mary Museum, which held a number of bequests from Garry Barenboim, the strange old man who once owned the house that contained the stone statue. On a reconnaissance trip earlier that day, Sam learned that Barenboim had left the museum gold knives and forks, eighteenth-century hats, a mammoth tooth, a crystal goblet said to have belonged to the explorer Jacques Cartier, and an Aztec necklace — all things Sam suspected the man had gathered via time travel. He had also left five coins with holes in their centers, coins of just the right size.

And that was how Sam came to be crouching in a dinosaur's rear end at ten o'clock at night.

When he was sure the guards couldn't hear him, he left his hiding place and switched on his cell phone, finding his way by the screen's bluish light. Velociraptor to the right, triceratops to the left: All he had to do was head straight toward the front desk, going as far as the local history hall. The coin case was at the far end of the room.

Shrouded in darkness, the museum was as unnerving as a haunted house, with dozens of threatening shadows that seemed about to bite. *Come on,* Sam told himself, *there's nothing alive in here, just dusty old stuff.*

And yet . . .

When Sam opened the door to the hallway, he thought he heard something like a key clinking against metal. He hid behind a statue of the sea god Neptune holding his pointed trident. Maybe one of the night watchmen had forgotten something. Going back was too risky, so Sam hunkered down, making himself as small as possible, and held his breath. There was a rustling noise on the floor, a flashlight beam in the next room, then nothing. Sam counted to a hundred before standing up. The coast was clear.

Hugging the walls, he reached the local history hall without any problem. There the entire story of Sainte-Mary was told in large dioramas. Costumed mannequins illustrating the town's different historical periods stood between each display. As Sam walked toward a milkmaid emptying her pail, he saw a shadow moving about ten yards away, by the coin room. A dark shape was leaning over a display case and fiddling with something that made a slight squeaking. Sam slapped his cell phone against his thigh to hide the light, but it chose just that moment to ring — or rather to vibrate, because Sam had wisely switched off the guitar riff he used as a ringtone. Except that in the heavy silence of the local history room, it sounded as if one of the wax figures had switched on its electric razor!

The shadow whirled around, the beam from its flashlight catching the milkmaid's plump cheeks. Sam crouched behind her pail as best he could, but it was too late. The burglar — the *other* burglar! — was already rushing at him. The man raised his flashlight to hit Sam, who was just able to dodge the blow by rolling to the foot of a mannequin of Gordon Swift, Sainte-Mary's first and most venerable mayor.

Sam barely had time to stand up before the man was after him again, and a furious scuffle followed: He punched, Sam ducked, he tried to knee Sam, Sam twisted away, Sam kicked out, the man parried the blow easily. All this was done in total silence, so as not to alert the guards. The man was powerful and apparently trained in this kind of hand-to-hand combat. He looked like a professional thief in a skintight black tracksuit, and he had taken the precaution of wearing a hood and gloves to hide his face and hands.

As Sam tried to grab him, he ripped the soft fabric of the burglar's tracksuit. The jerky light of the flashlight revealed a strange tattoo on his shoulder: a kind of U with flared ends and a big circle between them. The man must not have liked having his clothes torn, because he began hitting harder. He even managed to slip his hands around Sam's neck and gave a grunt of triumph as his thumbs started to crush his victim's Adam's apple.

With a sudden hip thrust he'd learned in judo, Sam knocked the man off balance, and the two of them tumbled into the legs of His Excellency Mayor Swift, who promptly toppled backward with a crash of shattered glass. The museum alarm system started to howl and the hallway lights came on. The burglar scrambled to his feet, releasing Sam. Blinded and choking, Sam glimpsed the hooded figure pause briefly at the coin case before racing out the door beside it. Over the howling of the siren, he heard shouts.

"He's headed for the front desk! Hurry!"

The guards raced past the local history room without stopping, and Sam forced himself to stand up. There might be a chance to turn the situation to his advantage. He rushed to the coin collection. The display case housing the Barenboim bequest was wide open, its lock forced, but he swore as he took in the situation. All the coins with holes in them had disappeared, except one that the thief in black must have missed. There were two burglars after the same treasure!

"He's going for the service entrance!" cried a night watchman.

They'll be coming back, Sam told himself. *They're sure to come back.* They would search every nook and cranny of the museum, and the Baryonyx's belly wouldn't be much help to him. He had to leave now. But the only possible way out . . .

Sam glanced down the hall. Empty. He pocketed the remaining coin, crouched down, and ran in the opposite direction from the fugitive, keeping his ears cocked. The alarm had fallen silent, and he could hear muffled voices. When he reached the front desk, he looked in every direction. The service entrance was over by the locker rooms. It opened onto a dark hallway, and he could feel a breeze: the exit!

Outside, the guards were yelling, "Stop, thief! The museum's been robbed!"

As Sam felt his way down the hall, he bumped against a door handle on the right-hand wall and turned it. From the smell, it was a room where garbage cans were stored. He leaped inside, knocking over a broom cart, and yanked the door shut. His heart was pounding and the rest of his body felt as if a train had run over him.

After a few minutes, the guards came back. They hadn't been able to catch the man in black.

"I'll . . . I'll call the police," gasped one, out of breath. "You try to see what he stole."

They walked down the hall without showing any interest in the brooms. Sam slipped silently out of his hiding place and quickly covered the last yards separating him from freedom. Fresh air! He ran down the steps, raced across a grassy rise, and sprinted to the corner without turning around. Taking streets at random, he didn't stop running until he'd put several blocks between himself and the museum.

It was only then that he realized he no longer had his cell phone.

CHAPTER TWO

Bad News

The next morning Sam pushed back his sheets and jumped out of bed — and immediately winced: His body was a mass of pain. Making his way slowly to the mirror, he saw that by luck his face had mostly been spared, except for a large bruise around his right eye. His alarm clock blinked 6:42, and he was tempted to go back to bed and rest.

Under the circumstances, however, he felt his bruises hardly mattered. From experience and calculation, Sam had determined that time passed seven times faster in the past than in the present, so a day here was the equivalent of a week when he was time-traveling. His father had been imprisoned for the last twenty of Sam's days, which meant he had spent almost five months languishing in some vermin-infested cell. Sam could imagine him frighteningly thin, huddled on a pile of sodden straw, licking water oozing down the walls or using his last strength to drive away hordes of hungry rats. How long could he hold out under those conditions?

Sam energetically rubbed his eyes and went to his closet to inspect the box with the few things he hoped might help him reach his father. One was the Book of Time, a handsome old volume with a cracked red cover whose pages, which were all identical, revealed the time-location of the last time traveler to use the stone statue. The book had shown Sam that his father was in medieval Wallachia, a prisoner of the murderous tyrant Vlad Tepes. Next to the book was a small plastic bag containing three examples of coins with holes that made the stone statue operate. One of them was clearly very old, with a writhing black snake embossed on the metal. As his father had left it for him before he disappeared, Sam thought the coin might have come from Vlad Tepes's time. The second was more recent and bore Arabic inscriptions. The third looked like a plastic poker chip with a hole. From under the bag, Sam took a sheet of paper with the text from an old book of spells he'd found during a "field trip" to Bruges, Belgium. The book had belonged to Klugg, an alchemist and all-around despicable human being. Its original text was in Latin, but his cousin Lily — with whom he was getting along better and better — had been good enough to translate it for him:

HE WHO GATHERS THE SEVEN TOKENS WILL BE THE MASTER OF THE SUN. IF HE CAN MAKE THE SIX RAYS SHINE, ITS HEART WILL BE THE KEY TO TIME. HE WILL THEN KNOW THE IMMORTAL HEAT.

The words didn't mean much at first glance, but for Sam the text was full of promise. His biggest problem was his inability to control his leaps through time. The jumps could be fifty years ago or five thousand — anything was possible. How could he ever reach his father under those conditions?

The Latin suggested that in order to get the key to time — and thereby choose the era you wanted to travel to — you had to get seven coins and arrange them properly on the stone statue, with the coin in the center of the carved sun indicating where you wanted to go, and the others placed in the six slits or rays that radiated out from it. Counting the coin Sam had picked up at the museum, he now had four.

The final item in the box was a bound book of photographs that Lily had borrowed from the Sainte-Mary Library. It was about Bran, one of many castles Vlad Tepes had frequented, and an illustration in it had caught her eye. It showed graffiti crudely scratched onto one of the dungeon walls: HELP ME SAM. The book's author had admitted to being perplexed. The photograph's caption read: "This graffiti was uncovered during the restoration of the Bran dungeon. According to some analyses, it is several centuries old. The fact that it is written in English adds to the mystery: Had Vlad Tepes captured one of the King of England's subjects during a military campaign? And who was this Sam the message was addressed to? Whatever the case, it provides further proof that it was not good to be a prisoner of the Prince of Wallachia."

When he thought about it, though, the graffiti actually made Sam feel hopeful. For some unknown reason, Vlad Tepes had decided not to execute his father immediately. Instead, he had sent him to cool his heels in one of his cells, which gave Sam some chance of finding Allan Faulkner alive. Moreover, if he had written those few words, it was because he saw Sam as the only person in the world able to get him out of there. He trusted his son, with a faith so exclusive and poignant that it put a huge responsibility on a fourteen-year-old's shoulders.

In a way, their roles had suddenly reversed: It was up to the son to look after the father. And despite the infinite sweep of time that separated them, Sam renewed his promise to Allan every morning: He would save him, whatever the cost.

Sam carefully returned his treasures to the back of his closet, then pulled on a shirt and some pants and went down to breakfast, moving slowly because of his bruises. He expected everyone to still be asleep, but Lily was already in the kitchen, hunched over a bowl of cereal.

"Lily, you're awake!"

"Since five a.m.," she whispered as she chewed. "I had a nightmare." She caught sight of his face. "Sammy, what happened?"

Sam grimaced. "I went to the museum last night to get the coins — only someone else got there first."

"You did? What? Who?"

"Let me get some breakfast," he said, pouring himself a big bowl of cornflakes. "What was your nightmare about?"

"Stupid stuff . . . You know Nelson, Jennifer's brother? I dreamed we were next to the swimming pool at their place, and he started to melt, like ice cream! First his feet got all soft, then his hands, and then his head started to drip. Jennifer was running around looking for ice cubes and yelling for her mom, but he kept on melting. In the end, all that was left was a little blue puddle, the color of his swimsuit. Stupid, isn't it?"

Sam took a spoon and stirred the cool milk, watching as a white sea swamped the golden flakes.

"Maybe not," he answered teasingly. "Maybe you want him to melt for you!"

Lily looked appalled. "Thanks a lot! Nelson is a total idiot! He can't say a sentence longer than four words, and his bedroom is covered with gun posters. Can you see me in love with a guy who decorates his room with guns? Besides, he's ugly."

Sam smiled slightly. He'd been very careful not to broach the delicate question of romance with his twelve-year-old cousin; he knew she'd let him have it. Besides, when it came to matters of the heart, his own record was pretty pathetic. The proof: For three long years he hadn't found the courage to go knock on the door of Alicia Todds, the only girl he'd ever loved. And when he'd finally seen her two days earlier, she'd been on the arm of a tall, arrogant blond boy. Smooth move, Sam!

"But if you were at the museum," Lily continued, "I guess you had something to do with this?"

She held out the *Sainte-Mary Tribune*. The headline on the front page proclaimed: "Strange Burglary at S-M Museum."

Sam took the paper and read it as he ate his cornflakes. The article didn't tell him anything that he didn't already know, and to his great relief it didn't mention his cell phone. Maybe it had fallen in a dark corner during the fight, and no one had picked it up. "The question of a motive remains open," concluded the reporter. "The thief or thieves went to a lot of trouble, but in the end all they took were a few coins of no great value."

"No great value for a *Tribune* reporter, maybe," he grumbled.

"Okay, Sammy, can I have your version now?" Lily said.

But before Sam could answer, they heard footsteps in the hall. "Meet me at the bookstore at eleven," he whispered just before Lily's mother, Evelyn, burst through the kitchen door, wearing a blindingly electric purple bathrobe.

"What did I tell you, Lily?" she screamed. "Am I talking Chinese or something? You're forbidden to be with your cousin till I say otherwise! He stole your phone three days ago, he wanders around God knows where with God knows who, and he won't give us the slightest explanation of any of it! Do you want to do the same?"

"I'm not doing anything!" protested Lily. "I'm eating my breakfast!"

"So why the whispers? What's he trying to put over on you now? You heard Rudolf's warning, didn't you? Sam is on a slippery slope, and for all we know, he's doing drugs! I'm warning you, Lily, if I have to be after you all the time, I'll send you to Camp Deadlake so fast it'll make your head spin!"

Aunt Evelyn seemed to be obsessed with lockups and discipline. Sam knew Deadlake was a summer camp famed for the strictness of its counselors — the female equivalent of the boot camp Evelyn had threatened him with recently. Now she turned and looked at him for the first time. "What happened to *you*?" she shrieked. "Did you get in a fight?"

"Evelyn, for heaven's sake! What are you talking about?"

Alerted by the shouting, Grandpa had hurried downstairs. His hair was sticking up every which way, and in his hurry, he'd buttoned his pajamas wrong — at sixes and sevens, as Grandma might say.

"What do you mean, what am I talking about?" said Evelyn, even louder. "Look at Sam! He has a black eye — probably because some drug deal went wrong!"

"Sammy, what happened?" Grandpa asked with real concern. "How did you get that shiner? Weren't you going to spend the night at Harold's?"

Sam had indeed told his grandparents that he was going to spend the night at his friend Harold's, even going so far as to have Harold agree to lie for him. He was sorry to drag Harold into it, but there was nothing else to be done.

"We went to the skateboarding park to do some aerials, and I went up for this really difficult jump. And then" — Sam tried to look embarrassed — "I guess I landed on my face. After that, I decided I wanted to come home to my own bed."

"I don't believe it," Aunt Evelyn declared.

Grandpa turned back to her with an exasperated expression. "And why not?"

"They were whispering when I came in. This damned boy is trying to suck Lily into more of his dirty tricks! He does nothing but plot behind my back!"

"Calm down, Evelyn," Grandpa ordered. "They're just children!"

"That's right, go on defending them! Just like Allan! You and Mom, you've always defended Allan! The poor little darling, right? He could do whatever he felt like! Come home at all hours, collect disgusting things, get bad grades — it didn't matter! But me . . ."

She heaved a sigh of rage.

"Anyway, you see what indulging all his whims has led to: He's vanished into thin air and left *you* to take care of his son! What you and Mom don't seem to understand is that Sam is going down exactly the same road, and you just close your eyes to it!"

Evelyn stormed out of the kitchen in a blur of purple sleeves, bumping past Grandpa as she headed for the hallway. Sam normally felt a pretty limited affection for this irritable aunt, who seemed angry at the entire world except for Rudolf, her boyfriend of the moment. But this time she had really gone too far. If he had the power, he would cheerfully send her and her ludicrous bathrobe to the Bran Castle dungeons to take his father's place. After all, maybe Dracula liked purple.

CHAPTER THREE

Seven Coins

Sam repressed a grimace as he pulled the bookstore curtains shut. Every time he lifted his arm, it felt as if a malevolent spirit were sinking an axe into his back. Luckily, his grandparents had believed his story about the skate park and had even offered to provide ice packs or heating pads for his bruises. But Sam had turned them down. Everything was fine now, he had said; everything was fine.

As soon as he was able to get free, he ran over to his father's antiquarian bookstore on Barenboim Street, more determined than ever to pursue his investigation. He especially wanted to discover the connection between last night's burglar, his mysterious tattoo, and the old coin he had overlooked. Sam took it from his pocket now. It was almost worn smooth, but you could make out a U with flared ends on either side of the central hole.

Overall, it looked a lot like the tattoo on the man in black's shoulder. A coincidence? Of course not.

Sam had searched the Internet to find something matching the symbol, but hadn't gotten a satisfactory answer because he wasn't able to frame the question clearly. But the mark resembled a hieroglyph, so Sam suspected that ancient Egypt was the place to look. As it happened, Faulkner's Antique Books was pretty well stocked in that area, so Sam planned to do a little browsing in the store, which he'd never bothered with before. As an extra advantage, he would be close to the stone statue for whatever might happen next.

Once hidden from prying eyes by the curtains, Sam carefully examined the sections that the bookstore devoted to history. Three shelves were given over to Egypt, each with several thick dictionaries and art and history books. After some browsing, he found what he was looking for in a nineteenth-century *Encyclopedia of the Pharaohs*. The strange U with a circle appeared in a chapter called "The Egyptian Pantheon." It was actually a pair of horns with a solar disk between them, and was an attribute of several gods and goddesses, among them Isis and Hathor, who wore a headdress resembling the symbol. The book didn't give many more details, but it confirmed Sam's hunch: ancient Egypt, the gods, the sun — all of these fit with the stone statue!

As he put down the encyclopedia, Sam noticed a small volume with a black dust jacket that must have been shelved incorrectly. It was a novel by an author he knew well, and for good reason: William Faulkner, one of the greatest American writers of the previous century. Allan practically worshipped Faulkner and was sorry not to have a family connection with

17

the man he called "one of the seven wonders of world literature." The book's title was appropriate: *Intruder in the Dust*. But how did this novel come to be in the history section?

Sam opened the book at random and got a surprise. The dust jacket didn't contain the Faulkner novel, but a small black notebook whose first pages had been torn out — at least fifty of them, to judge by the stubs still attached to the binding. His curiosity piqued, Sam inspected it more carefully. There were blank pages, more blank pages, and then a phone number. Sam thought for a moment and then went to the phone.

A pleasant voice answered his call: "First Canadian Bank of Sainte-Mary."

"Oh — oh, yes," Sam recovered, trying to make himself sound as adult as possible. "My name is Allan Faulkner, and I'm calling in regards to my account?"

"Oh, yes, Mr. Faulkner," the woman said. "What is your code word?"

"Elisa," Sam said, and spelled it out. It was his mother's first name, and a complete guess, but he heard keys clicking on the other end of the line.

"Well, you know, sir, that you have a significant mortgage payment due to us on your house."

"A mortgage payment?" said Sam blankly.

"Yes, Mr. Faulkner. The monthly repayment of your loan?" she said coldly. "Your payments are *five months* overdue. You have one more month. If you can't pay us the full amount then, we'll be forced to foreclose."

Sam sat stunned. From what he'd heard, foreclosure meant the bank would take over the house — and he couldn't let them have the stone statue!

"How much does my — how much do I owe?" he asked.

The woman named a sum that Sam was sure was far beyond anything in his father's bank account.

"I'll — I'll take care of that as soon as possible," he gasped and hung up the phone.

Sam would need to talk to his grandparents. Though he knew his father had been borrowing money from them for some time, they must have no idea of the extent of Allan's troubles — and he had no idea how they would cover this. But they had a whole month, and there wasn't anything he could do about it right now.

Sam pushed the matter firmly from his mind and went back to the little black notebook. There was nothing more written in it until the very last page, where Sam found a few words scribbled by his father, like a memo or a shopping list:

MERIWESERRE = 0
CALIPH AL-HAKIM, 1010
$1,000,000!
XERXES, 484 B.C.
LET THE BEGINNING SHOW THE WAY
V. = 0
IZMIT, AROUND 1400?
ISFAHAN, 1386

And at the very bottom, underlined twice:

BRAN

Bran, Vlad Tepes's castle! Where his father had gone! And quite deliberately, since he had taken the trouble to write his destination in the notebook!

Feverish with excitement, Sam read and reread the few lines, struggling to guess their hidden meaning. His father loved puzzles — everything from trivia quizzes to Rubik's Cubes to Sudoku — and it was possible he had left this as a coded message for Sam, but it was equally possible the list was just the jottings from some obscure piece of research. Dates, exotic names, figures . . . Sam racked his brain but couldn't come up with anything.

"Good grief, Dad," he cried in exasperation, "couldn't you have been a little clearer for once?"

"Talking to yourself?" asked a familiar voice behind him.

Sam jumped. "Lily! What are you doing here?"

"We had a date, didn't we? It's eleven o'clock, in case you haven't noticed."

"Eleven o'clock, right! I was thinking and . . . Are you sure nobody followed you?"

"I came in through the garden window, like you e-mailed me. Does this have to do with what happened at the museum?"

They sat down on one of the sofas that were supposed to make the Faulkner bookstore's clients — when by some miracle there were any — feel at home, and Sam described his adventures of the last eighteen hours in detail. His cousin listened carefully, nodding when he finished.

"Do you know who it could have been?" she asked.

"I'm not sure, but I have an idea."

"An idea?"

"Well, you remember what we found out about that archeology trip to Egypt twenty years ago, when my father found a stone statue in Setni's tomb? There was another intern the same age as him who was also involved in the excavation. And from what I understand, just like my dad, this intern would sometimes disappear for a couple of days."

"So what?"

"I'm convinced that the guy and my father discovered the stone statue together and they both used it."

"That was twenty years ago."

"Yes, except that when my father disappeared three weeks ago, someone left a weird message on the bookstore answering machine. It was a strange metallic voice, like it was disguised. It said something like 'Allan, can you hear me? Stop being a jerk, Allan, pick up!' Then when nobody answered, 'All right, I've warned you.' It was definitely threatening."

"What do you make of it?"

"This guy was looking for Dad, and I'll bet he wasn't trying to sell him life insurance. He seemed to know him pretty well."

"So you think it was this mystery intern from Egypt, and he's coming back now?" Lily sounded skeptical.

"It's just a guess, but I don't have any better ideas. The guy knows the whole story from the beginning, and he's already used the statue. Don't you think he could've gotten the bookstore address and tried to reach my father? Or heard about Barenboim and paid a visit to the Sainte-Mary Museum?" Sam paused. "Or worse, he could've spied on me."

"Spied on you?"

"I've been coming here every day for almost two weeks. It would be easy to see me and follow me!"

"Is that why you closed the curtains? And suggested I come in through the garden?"

"Just to be on the safe side."

"But if somebody's watching the bookstore, why meet here?"

Sam smiled grimly. "Because I've decided to make another trip, of course."

"You're kidding!"

"Do I look like I'm kidding? I have to go, Lily, and I need your help."

"But I thought that without the seven coins you didn't have any chance of finding your father! And you only have four, don't you?"

"Yeah, four counting the one from the museum. But think about the guy who used to live here, Barenboim. When he died, he left half a dozen coins to the city. And then there was the high priest Setni — I met his son Ahmosis in Egypt, remember?" Lily nodded. "When the archeologists searched around his sarcophagus at Thebes, they found coins made two or three thousand years after the tomb was sealed. How could medieval coins show up in an ancient tomb? Setni must have gotten those coins from different periods in time! And if I go traveling again, I'll be able to get some too."

"Wait a minute!" said Lily. "You told me you needed a coin to come back. Suppose you can't find one when you're there? Think about it! How would you get back? Isn't that what almost happened in Bruges?"

"This time I'll take care of that. I'll put a spare coin in the statue's cavity — the part that lets you transport objects. That way, no matter what happens, I'll always have a coin with me and be able to come back. That is, if you keep the Book of Time safe and you concentrate a little, of course."

Lily nodded slowly. During Sam's previous adventures, they had discovered that Lily could bring Sam back to the present if she happened to be thinking about him at the moment he touched the stone statue. She reached for the Book of Time in her cousin's backpack and opened it at random. Each page displayed the same engraving of the walls and steeples of the city of Bruges in 1430 — the time to which Sam had ventured last. "But if you use your emergency coin there, you'll lose it, won't you?"

"Yes, but if I just keep sitting around here, my father will die sooner or later. I need those seven coins, no matter what."

"All right," Lily said. "Go get your things and we'll meet in the basement."

Sam went upstairs to change. When he joined his cousin a few minutes later, he was wearing a shapeless cream-colored linen shirt and pants. It wasn't a very fashionable outfit, but unlike modern fabrics, the ancient material let Sam travel through time without losing his clothes.

Lily had already entered the secret basement storeroom that Allan Faulkner had created to hide the stone statue. She was perched on a yellow stool next to the cot, the only cheerful bit of color in the gloomy room, which was lit by an old-fashioned night-light.

"If Alicia Todds sees you in your new pajamas," she said, laughing, "she'll never look at you again!"

"Go ahead, laugh! Here, I'm leaving you these two coins." He handed her the plastic chip and the coin with the black snake. "When I'm gone, you'll find a third one next to the statue. Put all three in a safe place with the book and the notebook until I come back."

"Don't worry, I'm starting to get used to this," Lily said reassuringly. "But you've got to promise to be careful, okay? Avoid battlefields and crazy alchemists, especially. It won't do your father any good to have you stuck in the past."

"Cross my heart and hope to die," said Sam firmly. "First Viking I see, I'll run as fast as I can."

He was overdoing the self-confidence a bit, but there was no point in worrying his cousin.

"Well, when it's time to go . . ." he said to buck himself up.

He walked over to the statue, which was in the darkest part of the room. He could just barely make it out in the dim light, a vaguely oval stone about twenty inches high, completely ordinary-looking. As he knelt beside it, Sam felt a complicated mix of apprehension and eagerness, with the second overcoming the first. He also noticed that the two coins in his palm were getting warmer, as if heated by some invisible current. The process was beginning.

He decided to put the museum coin in the transport cavity and the one with Arabic writing in the center of the sun. It snapped into place perfectly, with a faint click: The stone must have some sort of powerful magnet built into it. A dull humming rose from the center of the statue, and the basement floor vibrated slightly. Sam turned toward Lily, but his eyes were already veiled with a kind of fog, and he could make out only her shape. He put his hand on top of the stone, and a wave of fire shot up his arm into his whole body.

CHAPTER FOUR

The Delphi Shepherd

Hunched over the short grass, Sam had the painful feeling that he'd been turned into a human torch, then shot through space at the speed of light. Yet his fingers, hands, and shirt-sleeves showed no burn marks. "You will know the immortal heat," the Bruges alchemist's old book of spells had said. It might have added: "And your guts will be turned inside out." Sam could feel his breakfast cereal fighting his stomach, determined to escape. By taking a few deep breaths, he was just able to repress his nausea.

"Aha! You're back!"

The voice came from behind him, and Sam turned around as quickly as his uncomfortable position allowed.

"Aw, I guess it isn't you!" said the voice with a touch of disappointment.

Ten yards away, a young man of about twenty was watching him curiously. He had dark, curly hair, and was wearing a patched old tunic tied with a string around his waist. He held a knobbed staff in his right hand, and apparently went around barefoot.

"Are you his son?" the young man asked, squinting as if he were straining to remember something.

Sam didn't react immediately. His first instinct was to look around for the stone statue. It stood nearby, fortunately, with the museum coin glinting brightly in its cavity. Sam took the coin and slowly stood up, feeling dizzy. He had landed in a dry, mountainous place, with thickets and scrawny trees growing between the rocks. The sea lay below in the distance. But which sea?

"Hey, won't you talk to me?"

The young man sounded annoyed, but Sam needed a few more seconds to gather his wits. He could hear bleating very close at hand, just on the other side of the hill. Was this guy a shepherd?

"I'm sorry, I . . ." Sam began. He paused before continuing, surprised by the unusually warm, melodious *os* and *oi* sounds of the words that sprang naturally from his mouth. Instant language ability was another inexplicable facet of the powerful magic worked by the stone statue. "I . . . I'm a bit lost."

The shepherd shot him a suspicious glance. "Your father told you to come, didn't he?"

My father, Sam repeated to himself. Could this be Vlad Tepes's era? Despite his slight remaining dizziness, he took a few steps toward the young man.

"My father? Do you — do you know my father?"

"You bet I know him! He did the same thing you did the other day."

The shepherd was pointing at the stone statue, which was half covered with weeds.

"You can tell me where he is, then?"

26

"If he told you to come, you must know that, don't you?"

"Er, yeah, of course," Sam agreed cautiously. "That is, more or less . . . What I don't know is *exactly* where he is."

The young man folded his arms on his chest and looked stubborn. "If you don't know that, it means he didn't tell you. If he didn't tell you, then you're not his son. If you're not his son . . ." He hesitated a moment before continuing: "Give me two ram's heads and I'll talk with you."

"Two ram's heads?" said Sam in astonishment. "I don't have two ram's heads!"

"He gave me two ram's heads, he did! If you don't give them to me, it's because you're nasty. If you're nasty, it's because you're not nice. If you're not nice, I won't talk with you."

Sam realized that the young man, despite being older than he was, still thought and spoke like a young child. The shepherd suddenly turned and ran off, singing as he went. "Yes, yes, he came! He sure did come! He had something to do, oh yes, something to do! He gave me two ram's heads!"

In spite of his stiff legs, Sam was forced to run after him. "Hey, wait! I have to find my father! It's really important!"

But the shepherd raced nimbly among the stones, and Sam, who wasn't used to walking barefoot, watched as he quickly disappeared into the bushes. When Sam reached the top of the hill, he saw a steep valley where some thirty goats were grazing. They looked up as they saw their shepherd racing toward them, still repeating his singsong: "I made pretty earrings from the pretty ram's heads. He's the one who gave them to me because he had something he had to do!"

Sam slowed to a walk and shouted: "Hey! I have to talk to you!"

The dog guarding the herd spotted Sam and rushed toward him, barking. A big ferocious animal with tawny fur, it stopped dead a yard from Sam and growled while its master cheered him on: "Aha! Argos will take care of the nasty man who doesn't want to give his ram's heads! Good dog, Argos, good dog!"

But contrary to what Sam feared, the animal didn't attack him. Instead, it slowly stretched out its muzzle and sniffed his calf. And when Sam extended his hand in greeting, the dog gave it a little lick.

At that, the shepherd's behavior changed completely. "Aha! Good dog, good for you! If Argos and you are friends, it means you aren't nasty. You may not be your father's son, but you're not nasty either. Good dog, Argos!"

Sam was able to walk calmly down the slope with the dog at his side, wagging its tail. It was all hard to believe. The air was warm and the sky a deep blue. The goats resumed their grazing. It could have been a stroll in the country on any beautiful spring day, except that Sam didn't know what part of the world he was in, and certainly not what time period.

When Sam caught up with the herd of goats, the young man spread his arms and then shook Sam's hand enthusiastically, as if they were meeting after an absence of many years.

"My name is Metaxos, and I wasn't sure you were coming as a friend. But Argos knew, didn't he? Follow me. I'll give you milk and honey and we'll share the hut, all right? Maybe you've come to look for something, right? And maybe after that . . ."

His eyes were shining, and Sam's heart sank. Metaxos reminded him of a bum he'd run into several times on Barenboim Street. Depending on his mood, he either insulted passersby or tried to kiss them. The town welfare service took him away one day, and he hadn't been seen since.

"I'm looking for my father," said Sam. "Do you know where he is?"

"Your father?" said the shepherd with a big smile. "What if he wasn't your father? Because if it was your father, he'd tell you where he was!"

"Vlad Tepes," continued Sam. "Does that name mean anything to you?"

"Vladtepes? That's a funny name, by the ram's horn! Not a name from around here, anyway. What's your name? I gave you my name, you have to give me yours."

"Er, Sam."

His answer seemed to fill the shepherd with joy. "Aha! Sam! Sam of the stone! Samos, yes, of course, Samos! Are you hungry, Samos? Come to the hut, I tell you. I'll give you milk and honey!"

Without giving Sam time to think, he whistled between his fingers to call his goats and began to drive them toward the bottom of the valley, while shouting incomprehensibly: "*Oldiloi!* Hey, *Oldiloi! Oldiloi!*"

Argos followed the herd, barking, and the whole menagerie raced down the hill at breakneck speed. The shepherd, the goats, the dog — they were all crazy!

Sam was soon left behind and had to hustle not to lose sight of the group, bruising his feet on the rough ground. After twenty minutes of an exhausting cross-country hike, he reached the edge of an olive grove. A rough wooden hut stood nearby. The goats had scattered among the trees and Metaxos was lighting a fire. There was no other house in sight.

"Where were you, Samos?" shouted Metaxos. "I thought you went back into your stone!"

"It's just that . . ." Sam gasped, "you're a little fast for me."

"Aha, of course! I'm the best shepherd in Delphi. Down there, they say, 'Metaxos runs like the wind!' "

Delphi, thought Sam. The name reminded him of something, but what? *I'll pay more attention in history class next year*, he promised himself.

The young shepherd wiped his soot-blackened hands and looked his guest over. "By the way, did you bring anything?"

"Did I bring anything?"

Metaxos shook his head, looking disappointed. "You don't really know enough to be his son! Why did you come here, if you didn't bring anything?"

"To find him! I'm looking for my father, I told you!"

"But he was dressed like you and at least three times older than you, for sure! I don't have a father, did you know that?"

"I'm really sorry, I —"

But the shepherd, his face somber, went on with his thought. "I don't have a mother either. No, no mother."

"I — I lost my mother too," admitted Sam, who was starting to wonder if he would ever get the information he needed.

"You lost your mother? How?"

"Well . . ." It was hard to explain that she'd been in a car crash three years earlier, and had died of her injuries after the car rolled down the embankment a couple of times — especially since Sam suspected he'd landed in a time when the wheel might not have been invented yet! So an automobile . . .

"She fell," he said. "From the top of a hill. A hill like that one."

"By Apollo!" exclaimed the young man in horror. "Hills are for picking flowers and herding animals, not for dying! You must be very sad, Samos. It's not the same for me. I don't know who to weep for because I never knew my parents. I was left on the steps of the great temple on the twelfth day of the month of Bysios. The priests took me in."

Priests, temple, Apollo . . . Sam was somewhere in antiquity. He was sorry he'd never learned to tell the Greek gods from the Roman ones.

"But it seems I'm not to live in the city," said Metaxos. "The priests made that clear to me. I'm like my animals. All I need is sky and grass, and my dog with me. But I'm a good shepherd, I am! The best in Delphi! And I always save my prettiest goats for the temple!"

Sam felt a wave of pity rising in him. Metaxos wasn't crazy; he was just terribly lonely.

"I have to find my father," Sam whispered quietly.

The shepherd suddenly seemed to understand. "Of course you have to find your father, Samos. You already lost your mother, so . . . Come on, come into the hut."

He took a burning stick from the fire and lit a small clay lamp near the door. They entered the modest dwelling, which was built of branches plastered with a rough mix of clay and straw. There were just two rooms. One had a stone fireplace in the center. The shepherd explained that he used the other room to pen animals that were sick or were about to have babies. If Aunt Evelyn had dropped in, she surely would have whipped out her air freshener: The place smelled like the monkey house at the Sainte-Mary Zoo.

Metaxos shone his light on a pile of things at the very back that at first glance looked like garbage — shells, bits of twisted metal, scraps of cloth — but that he seemed to prize.

"This is where I store my treasures! Look!" He bent over and pulled out some sharp fragments of a hard green substance. "You see, Samos! Your father left these here! Yes, your father!"

Sam held them up to the flame. Plastic, apparently. Pieces of green plastic. "Were there many of them?"

"Oh, more than I have fingers on my hands. It was afterward, when he came back here, that he crushed everything with his foot. And this strange pottery of his, it was everywhere. But I saw him do it, yes I did! I even saw what I wasn't supposed to see!"

"What did you see, Metaxos? You can tell me, can't you?"

The shepherd's face darkened. "No, no, I have to keep quiet. I promised. Silent as the grave, or else . . ." He glanced outside, fearful of being observed. Then he pointed at the pieces of plastic again. "But I can show you that, can't I, Samos? That's not the same, is it?"

"This is the thing my father brought with him in the stone, is that right?"

"Yes, yes! You must be his son, to know that! He came with that thing, all green!"

"Was there anything else?"

Metaxos hesitated. Then, while still watching the olive trees outside, he reached into the pile of bric-a-brac, pulled out a small metal rod, and handed it reverently to Sam.

"I heard the noise, you know. Oh yes, with my two ears! A noise that could only have come from the gods!"

Sam rolled the object in his hand. It was a drill bit, probably from a cordless drill, which wouldn't need to be plugged in once it was charged. What in the world had his father wanted to do with a drill?

"He gave you two ram's heads so you wouldn't say anything, right?"

Metaxos put his hand on his mouth as if he weren't allowed to answer.

Sam continued, "And it was the green thing that he brought that made so much noise? Did you get anything else from my father?"

The shepherd glanced furtively at the other side of the room. On a battered wooden chest — it looked salvaged from a shipwreck — stood a kind of doll dressed in gray cloth. Sam took the lamp and walked over. It turned out to be a clay statuette about six inches tall, a roughly female shape along the lines of a well-endowed lady wrestler, with a crudely sketched face.

"I made it myself," declared Metaxos proudly.

"It's very pretty. Is it a woman?"

"Oh yes, but it's more than a woman. It's my own mother!"

"Your mother? I thought your parents abandoned you."

"This is my new mother, the one who protects me. I mean my mother in Delphi. Sometimes I try to go see her, but I'm really not allowed to. Argos looks after the animals when I'm not here."

What he said was becoming more and more jumbled, as if the mention of his "mother in Delphi" upset him.

"What is she called?"

"She isn't called . . . well, not by her name. She's . . . she's the oracle, you understand?"

"The oracle?"

"Don't you know the oracle, Samos? The Oracle of Delphi? Your father, he knew about her."

"Oh yes, of course, the oracle," Sam recovered, without having the slightest idea what he was talking about. "I'm just a little surprised. The oracle, that's really somebody."

"That's for sure! But it's true that she's very fond of me. And your father made this tunic," he added, stroking the little statue. "He did a good job, didn't he?"

Allan must have done it to make friends with the shepherd — in addition to giving him two ram's heads that he had found God knows where. Because honestly, who travels through time carrying the heads of sheep?

"You can hold her if you like," added Metaxos. "She'll be good to you too."

Sam delicately took the small curvaceous figurine. Her dress was cut from a rough linen much like what he himself was wearing — further proof that his father had been there. As he turned the doll over, he noticed lines and dots on the cloth. "Did my father draw these?"

"Oh, yes. He's very good with his hands. Want me to show you?"

He untied the string that held the tunic on the statue and handed the cloth to Sam. Unfolded, the dress was a rectangle the size of a sheet of paper, with holes for the head and arms. A series of little squares was drawn on it in charcoal, with dots and letters that Sam couldn't decipher.

"Do you know what this means?"

"No. I don't know how to read. The priests tried to teach me once, but . . ."

The squares appeared to be houses lined up one after the other, with arrows and notes in some foreign writing. *It must be a map*, thought Sam, *with street names for landmarks*. He was about to ask if a neighborhood like the one pictured existed in Delphi when Argos began to bark loudly. Metaxos rushed to the door. A group of men armed with staffs was climbing the path to the hut.

"Hey, Metaxos, are you there? Don't be afraid, my boy. We mean you no harm. We just have some questions to ask you."

"It's the good priest," whispered the young man. "He's come looking for me! He thinks that . . . he thinks that . . ."

He wasn't able to finish, and his whole body was trembling.

"What does he think?" tried Sam.

But the shepherd only retreated deeper into his hut as the group approached.

"Ho, Metaxos! We know you're there! Your goats and your dog are here. Don't be childish!"

Sam decided he had better intervene. "He's here. He isn't hiding!" he called.

A half-dozen men were crossing the olive grove. They were all bearded and swarthy and wore the same kind of tunic as Metaxos, except that their tunics were clean. The oldest one, whose white hair fell to his shoulders, was probably the "good priest." He walked up to the door and looked at Sam. "Who are you?"

"I'm a friend of Metaxos. He's coming."

"I've never seen you around here. What is your name?"

"It's Samos," said the shepherd, suddenly appearing. "Yes, a friend of one of my friends. Samos of Samos!"

"Samos of Samos?" repeated the old man. "Your parents didn't have much imagination! But I want to talk to Metaxos. Come here, my boy."

He seemed annoyed by something, whereas the others looked stern. The priest put his hand on the shoulder of the shepherd, who lowered his eyes. "Metaxos, did you go down into the city three days ago?"

The young man stared at his bare feet, rocking slightly back and forth.

"Metaxos, it's very important for me to know. Did you go to town three days ago?"

The silence seemed to go on forever. All that could be heard was the buzzing of insects, the goats bleating a little distance away, and the quiet panting of Argos, who was lying under a tree.

"I think you were right, Lydias," said the old man with a sigh. "He must have been in Delphi that day."

"Of course I was right," exclaimed a short brown-haired man, waving his staff. "I saw him with my own eyes. He was prowling near the Treasury of the Athenians and —"

Metaxos suddenly bent down, slipped sideways, and tried to get away. But they all grabbed him at once, and he was soon collared and pinned to the ground.

"I didn't do anything, good priest!" he shouted as two men pulled him up, holding him tightly. "I'm a nice shepherd."

"See that?" shouted Lydias. "He tried to escape! That's certainly proof!"

"Metaxos," continued the priest in a patient voice. "Metaxos, listen to me and stop sniffling. Did you steal the Navel of the World from the Treasury of the Athenians? Yes or no? Tell me the truth, Metaxos. It's your only chance!"

His eyes full of tears, the shepherd looked at him. "I didn't do anything, good priest! I swear I didn't do anything!"

The priest shrugged in annoyance. "The archon will surely want to question them. It's too bad, but we have to take them to prison!"

CHAPTER FIVE

The Stranger

When Sam emerged from the valley and saw the city, it took his breath away. Delphi was a white pearl surrounded by stone, a majestic eagle's nest in the heart of the mountains. Houses with tile roofs clustered around gleaming structures whose angular facades shone in the sun. The scene was all the more striking because the town seemed lost in a world of cliffs and precipices. There were no villages or farms nearby, just jagged rock and empty sky.

Delphi may have been isolated, but it was hardly deserted. A dense crowd thronged its streets, and the yellow path snaking below it was jammed with carts and pilgrims.

After three-quarters of an hour of silent walking, Sam and Metaxos were escorted into a building guarded by soldiers with tall metal lances. They shoved the two prisoners into a windowless room in the back, with no furnishings beyond a few straw mats tossed on the ground.

"I'm going to get the archon," the priest said. "In the meantime, think carefully about what you are going to tell him."

He closed the door, and the two youths were plunged into darkness. Metaxos huddled in a corner, sniffling, and Sam stretched out on one of the mats. He was now positive that he was in Greece. Athens, Apollo, tunics, temples, columns — it all fit. But in what century? That was a mystery. From a conversation Sam overheard at the gates of the city between a soldier and a priest, he deduced that Delphi must be some kind of holy place where the Greeks came to consult the Pythia, or oracle, who gave his — or rather her — opinion on various questions. Like in *The Matrix,* except this was the original!

But far more important to Sam was that fact that his father had come to Delphi. Better yet, *he had come to Delphi just three days earlier.* Three Greek days didn't mean much in the big picture, of course; his father could have made the trip several months ago in his original time. Just the same, Sam had missed him by a hairsbreadth today. He imagined for a moment what such a meeting might look like. Once the first moments of astonishment and emotion had passed, they would find a quiet spot — in front of Metaxos's hut, say — and tell each other about their adventures. Allan would explain what had brought him to Delphi with a drill, and Sam would warn his father of the dangers awaiting him in Bran Castle. Together they would return quietly to Sainte-Mary — back to square one, and back to normal life!

Of course things hadn't turned out that way. Still, Allan's visit to Delphi gave Sam a new perspective on events. What if he really did meet his father during his time travels? It wouldn't be who his father was now, of course — it might be the college-aged Allan, when he was studying in Egypt, or the Allan of just a few months ago, when he was first beginning to use the stone statue again. Still, whenever it was that they ran into each other, all Sam had to do was warn him not to go to Wallachia in the future — and then there'd be no need to chase after the seven coins, or to go risking his life with Dracula!

But there was some bad news too, and it was called the Navel of the World. Sam didn't know exactly what that was, but he remembered the Sainte-Mary Museum guard's comment: "Did you read about that Greek thing they auctioned in London? The Navel of the World or some such. Ten million dollars in less than ten minutes!"

So the Navel of the World had recently been stolen in Delphi and even more recently — a few thousand years later, actually — sold in England. Between those two events, his father had come here with a drill. His father, whom Metaxos had surprised committing an act so reprehensible that he didn't dare talk about it. His father, who would lose the house, the bookstore, and the stone statue unless he could make an impossible mortgage payment. His father, who had become a thief — unless there was some other explanation.

"Samos!" whispered Metaxos. "Are you still here?"

"Of course I'm here," answered Sam, annoyed.

"Samos, I'm afraid. They're going to kill me."

"Don't be silly. They just want to know where the Navel of the World is. Can you tell me what it looks like?"

"You know less about it than your father," Metaxos remarked. "At least he —"

"All right, all right," Sam interrupted. "I know less about it than my father — I get it! Just be nice and tell me what it is."

"It's the stone that shows the center of everything, Samos! When Zeus wanted to know where the center of the world was, he sent two eagles flying from opposite ends of the earth. The two eagles met above Delphi. They dropped the stone. That's how we know Delphi is the navel of the world."

"And this stone — where is it exactly?"

"The original is in Apollo's Temple. But the Athenians carved their own stone and covered it with gold. They were going to offer it to the god at the great feast. They stored it in their Treasury in the meantime. That's where your father . . ."

He started sniffling again, and Sam instinctively reached in his pocket for a handkerchief. He found only the museum coin and the statuette's cloth dress.

"Can you tell me what happened three days ago, Metaxos? Did my father tell you something? Like what he planned to do with the Navel of the World?"

"No, no!" the shepherd protested. "If I talk, I'll never go to the hills again, never! I'll never see my goats again, or my dog! I won't talk about your father, ever!"

Just then, the door flew open. "Are you two finished moaning? Come along. The archon is here."

The soldier led them to an oval room with a domed ceiling. A fat man with a chubby face sat at a marble table, his arm shuttling rhythmically between his mouth and a bowl full of grapes. The white-haired priest was pacing behind him, looking angry.

"Ah," said the priest, as he saw them approach. "So, Metaxos, have you been thinking? If you are the thief, you better tell us right away, my boy, so we can get the object back as soon as possible."

The shepherd fell to his knees imploringly. "It wasn't me, good priest! By Apollo and Hermes, it wasn't me!"

"So who was it, then?" snapped the old man. "Several people saw you prowling around the Treasuries that day, and you left town at nightfall clutching something in your arms. Can you tell me what you were carrying so carefully?"

"Don't . . . no," babbled Metaxos. "I . . . I . . ." He could no longer say anything intelligible.

"Do you realize what we've done for you all these years?" exploded the priest. "Who took you in when you were just a squalling baby on the temple steps? Who raised and fed you, and gave you your goats? Is this how you thank us, by robbing our best ally's Treasury?"

He grasped Metaxos under the armpit and forced him to his feet. "Do you know what will happen if we don't find the Navel of the World, Metaxos? In three months the Athenians will take their things and abandon the city. The Thebans, Boetians, and Corinthians will go next, and then all the others! Delphi will be deserted, the oracle silenced, and you'll be pasturing your goats among ruins!"

Metaxos looked terrified. "Good priest, good priest . . . don't kill me! I didn't do anything!"

"Who is this boy with him?" asked the archon, without pausing in swallowing his grapes.

"A friend of Metaxos," answered the priest. "Samos of Samos, I believe. They were both at the hut when we caught them."

42

"Does he know anything?"

"Metaxos claims he only arrived this morning."

"Is that true, Samos of Samos?" asked the archon without looking up.

"It's true," Sam said in a voice that he wished sounded more confident.

"And you don't know anything?"

Sam summoned all the courage he could muster. He was about to try something risky, but there was nothing else to do if he wanted to get out of this quickly.

"I think Metaxos found out something and he's very frightened," he said all at once.

"No, Samos!" the shepherd protested. "Keep quiet or I'll never go back to my hills!"

Sam ignored him and instead took the statuette's dress from his pocket and held it out. "Metaxos picked this up when he came to Delphi."

The archon deigned to look at him for the first time. "What is it?"

"A kind of map, I think."

At a nod, one of the guards stepped forward and brought the piece of cloth to the marble table. The archon looked at it every which way while making a sucking noise, as if he had something stuck between his teeth, and finally spat out a seed.

"It's a map of the city, all right," he said. "Crudely drawn, with names: 'theater,' 'temple,' 'Treasury of the Athenians.' That last one is marked with a cross. You say Metaxos picked this up on the Delphi road?"

Sam nodded.

"What if he had drawn it himself, instead of finding it?"

The priest, who had approached, shook his head. "Impossible. We were never able to teach Metaxos to read, much less write. Moreover, the shape of the letters looks like the way Greek is written in distant cities, not here."

"Cities more distant than the island of Samos?" asked the archon, glancing suspiciously at Sam.

"Much more distant, yes."

"So the thief would be a stranger, is that right?"

"It would seem so. Besides, Metaxos would hardly need a map to find his way to the Treasury of the Athenians. He spent his entire childhood in that neighborhood!"

"That's true," admitted the archon. "In that case . . . Tell me, Samos of Samos, do you have any idea what could have so frightened your friend?"

Sam cleared his throat as discreetly as possible. He had to come up with a convincing lie while making sure Metaxos didn't contradict him — no easy task. He stared hard at the shepherd, trying to send brain waves: *Trust me! Just repeat everything I say!*

"From what Metaxos told me," Sam began, improvising wildly, "he saw the map, got suspicious, and went to the Treasury of the Athenians. But when he got there, someone attacked him and threatened to kill him if he talked."

"Someone? Did you see someone at the Treasury of the Athenians, Metaxos?"

The shepherd opened blank, staring eyes as if his brain were momentarily disconnected: *I'm sorry, the number you are calling is temporarily out of service. Please try again later.*

The archon leaped to his feet and raised his fist to Metaxos. "Did you see the thief? Can you describe him? Speak!"

"It was a man," shouted Sam, to keep the archon from striking Metaxos. "About fifty years old, with short gray hair, a square jaw, and blue eyes."

The description had simply popped into his head. It was different enough from his father's appearance that it wouldn't cause Allan too much trouble if he ever came back here. Sam quickly went on: "Metaxos wasn't able to tell me more because everything happened too fast. The man had a knife and almost stabbed him, I think."

"Is this true?" asked the archon, his fist mere inches from the shepherd's face. "Was that the stranger you saw?"

It took a few moments before Metaxos's gaze showed a flicker of life. Then he nodded slowly. "Yes, that's . . . that's what I saw."

"Why did you refuse to talk? We've lost valuable time!"

"I — I was afraid. The stranger's knife, yes."

Sam heaved a sigh of relief. Apollo and his fellow gods had apparently taken his side.

"When did this happen, exactly?"

"After . . . after consulting the oracle," murmured the shepherd, as if under the effect of a powerful drug.

The archon stepped back, and the priest smiled slightly.

"That seems to fit. The lock at the rear of the building was broken at about that time, at the changing of the guard. It didn't take the thief more than a few moments to enter the Treasury and seize the Navel of the World."

"We still don't know how he was able to break the bolt, though," remarked the archon, reaching for another cluster of grapes. "Besides, nothing proves that Metaxos wasn't the thief's *accomplice* — and the Athenians won't be satisfied with his good looks or his simpleton manners. If they aren't given proof of his innocence, they will demand that he be punished."

Metaxos began to moan softly, like a dog unfairly reprimanded by its master.

"There may be a way to provide that proof," the priest suggested. "A proof that the Athenians themselves couldn't argue with."

"I'm listening."

"If this boy is truly guiltless, the oracle will declare him innocent," said the priest. "Otherwise . . ."

CHAPTER SIX

The Oracle

Actually reaching the oracle turned out to be no mean feat. At the foot of the temple, a dense crowd jammed a walkway lined with trophies: six-foot-high vases and shields, inscribed white pillars, a gilded statue of a lion, a bronze palm tree with a glittering owl perched in its fronds, and so on. You would have thought the people were extras for a scene in *Ulysses Against Hercules*.

The area was so crowded that the arrival of Sam and Metaxos, surrounded by the archon, the priest, and two guards, didn't go unnoticed.

"No shoving!" shouted one man.

"In Apollo's name," complained his neighbor, "you can't cut in line ahead of us!"

"We've been standing here for two hours," agreed the first man. "Wait your turn or —"

"It's the archon," interrupted a woman behind them. "Be quiet!"

They climbed the sacred path, making their way as best they could among the grumbling faithful. The organizers of the temple had clearly forgotten to arrange for VIP access. As they reached the first steps of the temple, the priest spoke into Sam's ear: "The two men holding their helmets over there are Athenians. They are here to keep an eye on us, so watch what you say or Metaxos could pay the price. Here — when you enter, give this as an offering."

He put two roughly circular bronze coins in Sam's hand. They didn't have holes, but Sam couldn't help but be startled: Each bore the head of a ram with long, curving horns. Two ram's heads! That was what his father gave Metaxos to buy his silence: two coins of the local money.

"I must go speak to them," said the archon, who went to confer with the representatives of Athens. Meanwhile, over to the left, two temple attendants were splashing water on a goat and watching its reaction. Sam had heard the priest at the city gate explain this to the soldier as well: If the animal shook itself vigorously, it was a favorable sign, and the visitors could be admitted. As Sam's group was waved forward, one of the attendants recognized the priest and hurried over to him.

"Master, it's you! If we had only known! Come this way, we will —"

"No, Selemnos, it is important that we proceed by the proper stages. We are being watched," he added, glancing at the Athenians.

The attendant followed his gaze and seemed to understand. "Well, in that case, please be good enough to make your offering."

Maybe it was seeing the goat, but Metaxos's good humor

gradually returned. He started to hum as he threw the two coins that the priest had given him onto a cloth.

"I gave my two ram's horns too! They aren't as beautiful as my beautiful earrings, but I'm going to see the oracle!"

From a mental-health standpoint, things weren't looking so good.

They stepped under the portico, a soaring, sculpted marble canopy supported by massive columns, then entered the temple proper. The archon soon joined them, followed by the Athenians.

"We have reached an agreement. None of the four of us must approach the boys while the oracle renders her judgment. We will stand ten paces behind them and keep totally silent. Each will listen to the answer and submit to the verdict. If the words' meaning is not clear, we will ask the usual interpreters for their opinion."

"Who should speak directly to Apollo?" asked the priest.

"Our Athenian friends want it to be Metaxos himself. He was the first to be accused, so he must confront the god."

"And the other one?"

"Samos of Samos? Our friends have trouble believing his version of the facts. They wonder about his connection with the stranger. It is essential that he also be present."

"And what guarantee do we have that they will not be bothered afterward?"

The younger Athenian, whose sharp eyes had been scrutinizing Sam, came forward, his helmet clanking.

"The representatives of the most glorious of Greek cities have given their word. If the two suspects have not stolen the

Navel of the World, they will be free to go. This Athens has decided!"

The two boys were asked to step deeper into the temple, where a smell of burned wood and aromatic herbs reigned. A servant had them sit on a wooden bench in front of a white curtain, as if to watch a puppet show.

"She's going to come," Metaxos whispered, suddenly very excited. "She's going to come!"

"Do you know what you're supposed to do?" Sam asked.

"Of course! With the oracle, I'm never afraid!"

Sam would have liked to share Metaxos's enthusiasm. He knew he was innocent, but he was afraid the Pythia would suddenly declare his father to be the real thief — in which case, the best way to recover the stolen goods would be to imprison his son.

There was a rustling behind the curtain, and the servant nodded gently. "Apollo is prepared to listen to you, young men."

"Is that right?" the shepherd exclaimed. "Is the oracle there? Back there?"

"Metax?" hissed a low voice on the other side of the sheet.

The curtain parted slightly, and Sam saw a middle-aged woman in a gray robe looking at them in surprise. She had stepped down from a three-legged metal stool and was standing next to a wide crack in the ground — perhaps a scar from an ancient earthquake. Her part of the sanctuary was lit by torches, and in the shadows you could make out a tree, a twisted, bullet-shaped stone — the original Navel of the World? — and various other objects. When she saw the archon and the priest a few yards away, she snapped the curtain shut. It clearly wasn't usual for the oracle to show herself to her

50

visitors. But the servant acted as if nothing was amiss and tiptoed out.

Metaxos stood up. "Oracle! Oracle of Delphi! Breath of the god Apollo! Did Metaxos steal the Athenians' golden stone?"

He sat down and winked at Sam.

At first nothing happened except for a slight clicking of teeth, as if the Pythia was chewing on something. Then a strange swallowing sound was heard, and she seemed to spit on the ground — *like the archon*, Sam thought. *Everybody spits here!* After a short silence, a hoarse voice rose that would be hard to imagine coming from a woman's throat.

"Apollo, the god most beloved of the gods, has heard your request, Metaxos. Here is his answer: Does the lamb steal the grass it eats from the mountain? Does the bird steal the water it drinks from the fish? Metaxos has never taken anything except the air he breathes and the milk he drinks from his animals' teats. It is Apollo's pleasure to give them to him."

The oracle then fell silent. A second passed, then ten seconds . . . Sam wasn't sure he grasped the message's hidden meaning, but overall, things were looking pretty favorable. In fact, the good priest was the first to express his pleasure.

"So much the better!" he exclaimed. "We now have proof that —"

From behind the curtain, the Pythia cut him off. "Apollo's breath has not expired! There is something else that men must know!"

Sam shrank on his bench: His father was surely about to be accused!

"Apollo, son of Zeus, has many times crossed the sky in his golden chariot," the hoarse voice continued. "He follows the course of the sun and sets the rhythm of the day. He knows the value of time and of the passing hours. Men of Delphi, let the shepherd's friend depart. Let him depart now. May he return through the gate of days that led him here. But he must hurry: One of his people is trying to close it. Apollo has spoken."

Sam had no time to think about the warning, because the more suspicious of the Athenians was on him in three quick steps.

"Whoever you really are, Samos of Samos, it would seem the gods have decided in your favor. But don't celebrate too soon. We will catch the stranger one of these days, and when that time comes, believe me: He won't steal anything ever again."

An hour later, Metaxos and his dog were chasing each other among the olive trees, delighted to be together again. The shepherd put his hands on his forehead to make them into horns — like the Minotaur? — and head down, charged his dog, who was barking joyously.

"Don't you want to play with us, Samos?"

"Not now. I'm thinking."

Sam was leaning against a wall in the hut's shadow, trying to make sense of the Pythia's warning. Apparently the Greek gods — or at least those who traveled with the sun and knew about the passing of time — shared some idea of the high priest Setni's magic. Egyptian gods and Greek gods, all wrestling with the same eternal question . . .

"One of my people," Sam repeated to himself. Someone from his own time, probably, who was trying to close the gate of days. Was it to prevent him from traveling? To keep his father from returning? And how did you close the "gate of days," anyway?

"Come out and play, Samos!"

"Thanks, no. I have to leave."

Sam had been turning the coin in his pocket over and over. What if he spent an extra night here? The Treasury of the Athenians was so close; wasn't it likely that it held at least a few coins with holes in them? His father had done half the job by breaking the lock with his drill. If Sam was careful . . .

Argos suddenly bolted inside the hut, followed by his master, who tripped and fell to the ground, laughing. "Metaxos is going to eat you up, you hound from Hades!"

There was also that comment by the Athenian representative: "We will catch the stranger one of these days, and when that time comes, he won't steal anything ever again." Did that mean his father had stolen other things from this time besides the Navel of the World? And that he could be expected to return soon? Who knows — maybe if Sam stationed himself by the stone for a while, he would see him reappear!

"Here, Samos, this bread is for you."

A sweaty Metaxos emerged from his poor shelter, holding a nearly whole round loaf under his arm. He gave Sam a slice a handbreadth wide.

"This is the Navel of the World," he added with a sly look.

"I'm sorry?"

"This is what I was hiding the other night when the guards saw me leaving the city. A nice loaf of bread my Delphi mother gave me; a nice loaf she baked for me! But you mustn't ever tell anyone that the oracle takes care of Metaxos, all right? It would shame her, since I'm just a shepherd. That's why I had to keep quiet."

Sam was astonished. "The Athenians could have had you put to death," he said. "You risked your life so you wouldn't betray your Delphi mother?"

"I was right, since Samos came," he answered candidly. "The gods rewarded me well. For that matter —" Metaxos put his other hand in his pocket. "You deserve a reward too. You can give these back to your father."

He held something out: Dangling from wires were two coins with holes in them. *Two coins with holes!*

"These are the pretty earrings your father made with the ram's horns. He gave them to me before the stone swallowed him."

Sam laid them cautiously in his palm. Two coins, the right size and with nice holes in them, mounted as pendants and bearing the ram of Delphi. His father must have stolen them from the Treasury of the Athenians.

"I'll give one back to you, anyway," Sam blurted, trying to master his emotion. "You can pick it up next to the stone after I'm gone."

"That way I'll have a souvenir of both of you!"

"Yes, and I'll have a souvenir of you."

All that remained was for Sam to leave for good. Metaxos let him understand that he didn't want to accompany him to the stone statue, and that he would retrieve the precious coin later. Indeed, the shepherd seemed almost relieved to see him go, as if the threat of being torn from his hills and sucked into nothingness would disappear with Samos of Samos. He barely waved good-bye, just turned his back to go tend his animals. Was that a way of making the farewells easier?

Sam climbed back up the hill toward the meadow where he had arrived only that morning — an eternity ago! In the distance, the sun was setting on the glowing sea, and he saw a black dot racing above the waves. Was it Apollo's chariot, crossing the sky at the end of the day? After all, nothing was impossible.

CHAPTER SEVEN

A Rabid Rabbit

Sam lay on the basement's cement floor for a moment, catching his breath. Aside from nausea, one of the most uncomfortable effects of his trips was the echo effect he experienced on his return, where every sound and movement around him was repeated with a slight delay. This déjà vu effect had been invaluable when he faced big Monk during the Sainte-Mary judo tournament the previous week, because it let him anticipate his opponent's moves and eventually win the championship. But it was very unsettling, and Sam spent several minutes waiting for it to wear off.

He then left the secret storeroom, taking care to pull the tapestry that hid the entrance back in place. The bookstore was empty, and he was able to change his clothes — nothing like a good pair of jeans! — before wolfing down a chocolate bar that he had thought to stash in one of the kitchen cabinets. He then climbed out the ground-floor window and crossed Mrs. Bombardier's and the Fosters' backyards. The Fosters' dog, who was usually pretty friendly, bared its teeth at him; maybe it caught a whiff of its distant Greek forebear.

After making sure Barenboim Street was empty, Sam hopped the fence and took the bus to his grandmother's, praying that Aunt Evelyn wouldn't be home. Alas, Apollo must have withdrawn his blessing en route. Sam had barely gotten off at the bus stop when a brand-new Porsche 4×4 drove up onto the sidewalk, heading straight toward him, and stopped in a squeal of tires a foot away. Evelyn's boyfriend Rudolf — that's what she called him, "my boyfriend," even though at fifty he was long past being a boy — jumped out.

"Well, well, if it isn't Samuel! Mind telling me where you're coming from?"

"Is that any of your business?" Sam said coldly.

The passenger-side window came purring down, and a familiar voice rode a gust of air-conditioning out of the car.

"Of course it's his business, you rude thing!" screeched Aunt Evelyn. "Someone has to be concerned about how you spend your days! If your father hadn't disappeared and forced your grandparents to —"

"That's all right, darling," said Rudolf. "I'll deal with him."

He strode toward Sam as if he were about to give him the beating of the millennium. Ever since Allan Faulkner had disappeared, Rudolf had shown an unfortunate tendency to view himself as the head of the family, and to see in Sam a particularly intractable future delinquent. He had first suggested the boot camp in the United States for Sam not long before.

"You didn't have lunch with Grandma, did you? She left to play bridge just now and was wondering where you'd gone to."

"I let her know," replied Sam. "I was at Harold's all afternoon."

"Harold, eh? He's very convenient, Harold is." Rudolf's glittering blue eyes looked anything but friendly. "Tell me, what did you do to your aunt this morning?"

"This morning?"

"Yes, when you were trying to involve Lily in your dirty little tricks. You got Grandpa upset at Evelyn."

"What?" shouted Sam. "She's the one who got hysterical! We were just eating our cereal when —"

Rudolf drew back his hand and seemed about to hit him. "Don't *ever* speak about your aunt that way!"

Sam was about to defend himself when he noticed Lily waving wildly at him from the back of the car. He didn't understand what his cousin was trying to tell him, but he figured that a fight with Rudolf would only cause her extra problems. So he stepped back and lowered his eyes.

"That's better," Rudolf snapped, mistaking his reaction for submission. "Don't you know your aunt has weak nerves? She's very sensitive to being called hysterical. And your father hasn't always behaved well toward her. In fact, it's partly *his* fault that she's in the state she is. So if you're planning to go the same route, you'll have to deal with me."

Sam shrugged and held his tongue.

"We're going to spend the night at a hotel near the water park. When we get back, I don't want your grandparents telling me you've gotten into trouble again. All right?"

Sam nodded slowly. He was only half listening to Rudolf rant because he was trying to understand the charades Lily was acting out in the backseat. First she drew something in the air: a rectangle . . . a rectangle that you unfold . . . a book . . . the Book of Time, for sure! Okay, what next? She slipped her right arm under her left one, then put both hands above her ears and began to wiggle them while shaking her head . . . A rabbit? What did a rabbit have to do with anything? She also opened her mouth in a funny way, as if she were trying to bite. . . . A crazed rabbit that hopped out of the Book of Time? It didn't make any sense!

But Evelyn was raising her window and Sam couldn't see anything more through the tinted glass. Rudolf walked back to the car, pointing his finger at him. "Don't you give your aunt a hard time, boy, ever again!"

He slammed the door and roared off, probably pleased by his show of strength. Rudolf really was a self-satisfied idiot.

When Sam got to his grandmother's, he first checked to make sure he was home alone, then attacked the refrigerator. He stacked a tray with a big glass of orange juice, two slices of cold pizza reheated in the microwave, the remains of a pasta salad, a piece of cheese so artificial that the milk it was made of probably came from a plastic cow, two chocolate yogurts, and a nice red apple that he polished with his napkin. He carried all this to the table and devoured it at a speed close to the world snacking record.

His hunger satisfied, Sam went up to his room, pulled on a clean T-shirt, and rummaged in his closet for the hidden box. He found the collection of photographs of Bran Castle and the sheet with the alchemist's Latin text, but not the Book of Time or the coins. Lily hadn't put them back, apparently. Was that what she was trying to tell him in the car?

He hurried to her bedroom next door, a place he didn't often have occasion to enter. Before discovering the stone statue, Sam and Lily had avoided each other as much as possible, each viewing the other as a living monument of purest stupidity. Their time-travel adventures had brought them much closer, but hadn't given Sam time to visit his cousin's domain.

A very strange place, a girl's bedroom — all mauve and pink, from the bedspread to the curtains, and including the pillows, lamp, bandanna on the chair back, book bag, and dance slippers. Orlando Bloom ruled the appropriately lavender walls: Orlando Bloom as an elf, Orlando Bloom as a pirate, Orlando Bloom as a Trojan warrior, Orlando Bloom sitting with his legs crossed, Orlando Bloom standing with his arms crossed, Orlando Bloom lying down with his fingers crossed. He was clearly a full-time demigod.

All right, wondered Sam, *where could she have put them?*

He opened closets, looked under the bed, and parted the curtains: nothing. He moved books, pulled out the bookcase, and felt behind the chest of drawers: nothing. Zan, Lily's favorite stuffed animal, lay on one of the stereo speakers and seemed to be mocking Sam's efforts. He was a floppy dog with short gray fur, a pointed snout, and long, dangling ears. *Ears!* His cousin wasn't pretending to be a rabid rabbit, but her pet pooch! *Arf!*

Sam grabbed Zan and shook him, but the dog was too small to contain a book. He then inspected the speaker Zan had been on, tipping it back and forth. Sure enough, something moved inside. He gently removed the black screen covering the loudspeaker and — bingo! — out slid the Book of Time and his father's black notebook. The three coins with holes were neatly taped inside the speaker case. Sam carefully replaced the screen. His cousin might have dubious taste in colors, but when it came to hiding places, she couldn't be beat!

Sam waited until he was back in his room to open the big red book. The same title appeared on every page: "Delphi, the Sanctuary of Apollo." Two black-and-white engravings showed the ruined city from above and the Temple of Apollo with its few remaining upright columns. The text recounted a legend in which Apollo had to defeat a terrible serpent before establishing his temple and his cult. There was also a reference to the Navel of the World, or *omphalos*, the famous stone that the two eagles dropped to mark the center of the earth.

The omphalos . . .

Sam sat down at his computer and launched an Internet search. He wasn't so much interested in the history of the omphalos as in what had happened to it recently. He found a few photographs of the stone — it was indeed bullet shaped, the way it had looked behind the temple curtain, with braided ropes carved on its sides — and some articles that confirmed his hunch. The original of the Navel of the World was on display at the Delphi Museum, but a number of copies of it existed. One long-missing gold copy had recently turned up and been auctioned in London for the equivalent of $10,125,000. The seller was Arkeos, a private company that specialized in high-end antiquities. It reportedly received the piece from an anonymous collector whose name it had agreed not to reveal; the buyer was a major Japanese bank.

Sam clicked on the arkeos.com link and swore under his breath when he saw the company's home page appear. Arkeos's logo was a pair of tapering horns enclosing a solar disk — the same strange U as the one tattooed on the burglar's shoulder!

How could that be? Unless . . . Sam dreaded what he was starting to suspect. Had his father stolen the Navel of the World in order to sell it to Arkeos? Was he perhaps in league with the thief at the museum? If the thief had been an archeology intern with Allan in Egypt, they might have been friends — but then he probably wouldn't call and threaten Allan, nor would he beat up Allan's son! Of course, according to Sam's theory, the other intern also knew how to time-travel, so he could have stolen the omphalos himself. But where would he have found a stone statue? As far as Sam knew, the Barenboim house sheltered the only one in Sainte-Mary — in North America, as a matter of fact. And Metaxos had been so certain that his visitor with the ram's heads was Sam's father.

"What kind of a mess did you get yourself in now, Dad?"

But Allan didn't answer him, any more than he had that morning.

Sam opened the black notebook and scanned the odd list again.

MERIWESERRE = O
CALIPH AL-HAKIM, 1010
$1,000,000!
XERXES, 484 B.C.
LET THE BEGINNING SHOW THE WAY
V. = O
IZMIT, AROUND 1400?
ISFAHAN, 1386

It still didn't make much sense, but thanks to the Web, Sam learned a little more about each of these things. Meriweserre, whose name was spelled several different ways, was an Egyptian pharaoh of the fifteenth dynasty. Al-Hakim was a Middle Eastern ruler around 1010. Xerxes was a Persian emperor who fought the Greeks. Izmit and Isfahan were cities, one in Turkey and the other in Iran. Had his father gone to all those places and all those times? Or was he planning to go there? And what was the connection with Bran Castle?

As for the rest of the message, only the money amount made sense. Was Allan supposed to receive a million dollars as a commission on the Navel of the World sale? Or was it the value of some other archeological treasure he planned to steal? A million dollars would certainly pay off the mortgage, allowing him to continue time-traveling — and to continue stealing antiquities.

Sam decided to store all the information he'd gathered in his computer. As he copied a picture of the omphalos into his images folder, he came across the family photo album he'd scanned a few years earlier. He usually avoided looking at it, because the past was still too painful. But today, after everything he'd learned — including the mounting evidence that his father was a thief— Sam wanted to look back at that wonderful time when he had both his parents and no harm could ever reach him.

Feeling heartsick, he stared at the screen. The slide show ran through their big Bel View house; Allan feeding him a baby bottle; his mother laughing at the county fair; a Christmas tree surrounded by presents; his first bicycle; a group shot, again with his mother, who was hugging him tight. . . . It felt both wonderful and unbearable.

The next photo showed him building a snowman with Alicia. The picture must have been taken right after the Todds moved in next door, since he and Alicia looked about nine years old. From then on, Alicia's sweet face, blond hair, and big blue eyes appeared along with Sam more and more often. For two years they had been inseparable: same school; same friends; same books, whose chapters they read aloud to each other; same movies, whose favorite scenes they would endlessly reenact; same hysterical giggles when their parents came upstairs to make sure they were asleep.

Then Elisa Faulkner had died, and a black shroud fell over everything. Sam had felt he was tumbling into a bottomless pit, a well of sadness and bitterness that he couldn't escape without severing the sorrow that still connected him to his mother. He hadn't wanted to see anybody, not even Alicia. In the space of a few weeks he'd broken everything off.

Three years passed that way. The Faulkners moved out of Bel View, Sam changed schools, and even though he thought about Alicia all the time, he'd never had the courage to see her again. Until three days ago, in fact, at the judo tournament, when she'd appeared on Jerry Paxton's arm. The tall boy's presence and the festive mood in the gym made Sam feel awkward, and he hadn't been able to tell Alicia what was really in his heart: that his love for her hadn't changed, and that just by looking at him, she could tell it never would. There were a lot of things Alicia needed to hear, including the apologies Sam owed her, which he had left too long unsaid. And this time, waiting another three years was out of the question.

Sam looked at his watch. It was four-thirty. Maybe Alicia would agree to see him.

CHAPTER EIGHT

Alicia Todds

Sam hadn't been back to the Bel View neighborhood in ages, and when he saw the first white colonial-style houses with their big lawns, he felt almost dizzy. Everything was the same, yet everything was so different! The maple trees that lined the avenue, the colorful bushes and flower beds, the blue mailboxes by the paved walkways, the sidewalk where he first learned to skateboard — well, where his knees and elbows first learned — the lamppost he had swung around so many times . . . Except that he wasn't ten years old anymore, the bus hadn't just dropped him off after school, and his mother wasn't waiting with a grapefruit-orange juice cocktail ("It's full of vitamins, Sammy!") and his favorite cookies. Today he was a stranger: a stranger to his childhood, a stranger to his neighborhood, a stranger to what he might have become if everything hadn't changed.

Sam stopped to let his heart slow to a normal rhythm. His house — his old house — was the third from the corner, the one with the green window trim. Alicia's was next door. Number 18, where he was standing, belonged to Miss Maggie

Pye, who had occasionally babysat for him when he was little. As it happened, she was standing over her rosebushes, garden clippers in hand.

"Miss Pye?" he called over the fence.

She turned, probably surprised not to recognize the voice. "What can I do for you?"

"It's me, Sam. Sam Faulkner."

"Sam Faulkner?" she said, adjusting her glasses. "Good heavens, it's Sammy Faulkner!" But she didn't make a move to come greet him. "I wouldn't have recognized you! What are you doing around here? You must have moved away three or four years ago, eh?"

"Yes, three years ago," said Sam. He felt a bit disappointed by the chilly welcome, but after all, what had he expected? That the neighbors would rush into the street, setting off fireworks and yelling, "Hallelujah! Sam's back!"?

"It was a real tragedy," said Miss Pye with a sigh. "Still, you grow up, you get over it. At your age you have other things on your mind, don't you?"

She stood there smiling tensely, her free hand resting on her flashy jeweled necklace. Miss Pye was so fond of jewelry that Allan had dubbed her "Miss Magpie" — irresistibly drawn to anything that gleamed, clinked, or sparkled. Sam wondered if she thought he wanted to steal her precious necklace.

"Well, see you next time, Miss Pye."

"Okay, see you then."

She turned back to her roses as if nothing had happened. Sam felt especially let down because in the old days they had all liked each other. When he had his appendix out, for example, Miss Pye had dropped by the hospital to say hello and even brought him a box of candies. True, she had devoured them while he watched, but then, she never could resist treats wrapped in shiny paper!

And then later that day, his mother had set out for the hospital in her car, and crashed down the embankment.

Swallowing his sudden sadness, Sam briskly walked up the path to the Toddses' house and pressed the doorbell. A few moments later, the door opened.

"What can I do for you?"

It was Helena Todds, Alicia's mother. She was almost as beautiful as her daughter, with the same golden hair, but her features weren't quite as defined. She was also shorter than Sam remembered.

"Are you looking for something?" she asked in a friendly way.

"I — I'm Sam Faulkner," he stammered.

Helena Todds's eyes widened. "Sam Faulkner! Of course! Sam!" She gave him a big hug and kissed him firmly on both cheeks. Sam could feel something melting in his chest. "You're all grown up now! You're handsome too, just like your father! And almost as tall, aren't you? Let me guess: You're on vacation from school, so you decided to drop by."

"That's right. I — I had a question I wanted to ask you."

Helena Todds seemed amused by his embarrassment. "Did you come to see Alicia? She's out now, but she should be home soon. I gather you ran into each other at the judo tournament."

Alicia had mentioned him to her mother! *Alicia had mentioned him to her mother!* His mood brightened immediately. "I was really happy to see her," he admitted.

"And you won too! I'm so pleased you're doing well after all these years! But come in, come in!"

Sam followed her through the hallway into the living room, which was furnished in the same nautical theme he remembered: antique charts on the pale wood walls, a big mahogany bookcase, and navigation instruments scattered here and there. Sam sat down on the big leather sofa next to a low table, where his parents had so often sat when they came over for a drink.

"What about your father? How is he?" asked Helena.

"He's . . . he's traveling."

"Oh, good. On business, right? Is the bookstore doing well?"

"Er, yes. At least it's starting to."

"I think Allan has a good reputation among collectors, and that's something! You know, we worried a lot about you," she added more quietly. "I mean after your mother's death. Allan just shut himself up. He didn't want to go out anymore or talk or see us. . . . I think we should have insisted that he not be alone. Forced him, even! I felt guilty about that afterward, if only for your sake. It isn't good for an eleven-year-old boy to find himself all alone at home after . . . Anyway, I feel I didn't really do what I should have. I hope you don't resent me for it."

Sam was speechless. From his point of view, *he* was the one who had walled himself up in his sorrow — like his father — and kept anybody from distracting him from it, even Alicia.

"Don't worry, Mrs. Todds," he finally answered. "Everything's fine now."

"Including that black eye you're sporting?"

Sam had forgotten about it. "Oh, that's just from the tournament."

"Well, that's better," she continued in a more cheerful tone. "What was the question you wanted to ask?"

A question? Sam wondered. Oh yes, his supposed reason for coming over!

"Well, it's strange, actually," he said, thinking fast. "There was a show about Flemish painters on TV the other day, and I watched it because art is one of my favorite subjects at school. Anyway, I don't know if you're going believe this, but they showed a painting that you'd swear was of Alicia."

Helena spread her hands, not understanding. "It must be a coincidence!"

"That's what I thought at first, but later in the broadcast they said the young woman had been painted by her father, Hans Baltus, and that she married a man named Van Todds."

"Van Todds! That's funny, because I think Mark's great-grandfather was called Van Todds! He lost the Van while crossing the Atlantic. But he did come from there, from Belgium. And if I remember right, there were some painters in the family. What did the painting look like?"

Sam thought back to the day when Alicia's ancestor Yser had posed in Baltus's studio in Bruges, with its smell of oil and camphor. Sam had merely finished the portrait by painting the young woman's hands, but he felt quite proud of the result.

"It was . . . It was very good. The model wore a beautiful black velvet dress with a hat, and —"

The ring of the front doorbell cut him off.

"That must be Alicia; she always rings. Come on, we'll surprise her."

They hurried to the door, which opened to reveal Alicia on the stoop. But she wasn't alone: Jerry Paxton had his arm around her shoulder. Sam, whose heart had earlier melted, now felt it suddenly freeze. Alicia looked at him in surprise and Jerry scowled.

"What are you doing here, Faulkner? You get lost or something?"

Helena spoke up. "It seems to me I can invite whoever I like to my house, Jerry."

Paxton made a vague gesture of apology. He said good-bye to Mrs. Todds, kissed her daughter on the cheek, and walked away, grumbling to himself.

"Thanks a lot!" Alicia said to her mother once she was inside. "Now Jerry's going to sulk for the next two days!"

"If he doesn't like you having your friends over, you better get him used to it right away," replied her mother. "Anyway, now that you're both here, I'll leave you alone. I have some errands to run for your brother, Alicia. He's going to Grandma's tomorrow and I have to buy him some shirts. Sam, I'm really happy you dropped by. If you ever need anything, you let me know," she said with a serious look. "And come back whenever you like!"

She kissed him warmly while Alicia ran up the stairs. It was only at the top that the lovely girl deigned to turn around and look down at Sam.

"What are you waiting for? Aren't you coming up?"

Alicia's room was nothing like Lily's: no pink anywhere, no Orlando Bloom as an elf, no menagerie of stuffed animals. Instead, there were dozens of black-and-white photographs on the walls: landscapes, street scenes both crowded and empty, farm machinery, animals, close-ups of fruit, self-portraits, schoolmates, and an enlarged picture of Jerry above the bed.

"You do photography?" asked Sam.

"For a while now, yeah."

After an awkward silence she went on. "Do you remember when we ordered pizzas for Mr. Roger across the street?" she continued. "I took pictures of the deliveryman and the way poor Mr. Roger looked with fourteen pizzas he hadn't wanted. I guess it started with that."

Sam remembered the episode very well, including the fact that when Alicia's pictures were discovered, they earned her a memorable punishment.

"Well, they're really nice — congratulations!"

He wanted to praise the pictures enthusiastically, express his admiration with the right words, and all he could come up with was "They're really nice — congratulations!"? Pathetic.

He settled uneasily on the edge of the bed as Alicia slipped a White Stripes CD into the player. She sat down in a small red armchair and looked out the window at the garden while Jack White faced the Seven Nation Army, guitar in hand.

At the third verse, Alicia finally spoke. "What exactly do you want, Sam?"

"What do I want?"

"Last week you came over to talk to me at the gym. Today you show up here at the house. You haven't spoken to me in three years and now suddenly you're all over the place. So I'm asking: What do you want?"

There was no reason for this meeting to be easy, of course. But where to start?

"I'm really sorry," he began. "I don't have any excuse — I mean, I don't have any *good* excuse. All those years, I felt like if I allowed myself even a minute of happiness, it was like I was betraying my mother. I had to suffer, you know? At least a tiny piece of what she suffered. I got that in my head and —"

"What about me?" she asked angrily. "What was I supposed to do during that time?"

"I'm really sorry, Alicia. I couldn't help it."

"You know what I thought? That maybe you held me responsible for your mom's death. You were at my house for a sleepover the night you got appendicitis, remember? If I hadn't insisted you stay that evening, maybe you wouldn't have gotten sick. You wouldn't have gone to the hospital, your mom wouldn't have had to take her car to go there, and . . ."

She was clearly trying to keep a lid on her feelings, which seemed as sharp as ever three years later.

". . . she wouldn't have had the accident," she concluded.

"That's crazy!" protested Sam. "Totally crazy! I would never think something like that! You had nothing to do with it! If it was anybody's fault, it was mine! I shouldn't have gotten sick! I should've hung on, been stronger, that's all!"

He stopped, surprised by what he was saying. Was there a part of him that actually felt responsible for his mother's death?

Alicia was studying him from her armchair, less coldly now. To Sam, she looked even more beautiful.

"You see what happens when you keep it all inside, Sam? I was hurt, you know; I was really hurt. I loved you, and I'm not ashamed to say so. The way a little girl loves her Prince Charming. And you were my Prince Charming. Then all of a sudden, *pfft!* As if I didn't exist anymore. I was gone, scratched off the map. I'm sure it was horrible for you, but it wasn't much fun for me either."

Silence fell between them as Jack White sang with conviction, "I don't know what to do with myself." Sam didn't know what to do with himself either.

"Listen, Sam, don't be angry, but I'm not ready to see you again. Not now, anyway. Besides, there's Jerry. He's jealous, as I'm sure you noticed. Maybe later . . ."

She gave him a thin, pained smile, and Sam suddenly realized what a terrible waste those lost years represented for the two of them.

CHAPTER NINE

Pursued by a Bear

The next morning, as Sam climbed through the Faulkner Bookstore's back window, he was still filled with Alicia's face and words; his heart felt almost bruised by their reunion. When he crossed the hall, it took him a moment to process what he saw in the main reading room — and then he stopped dead. The place looked as if a hurricane had hit it. The curtains were thrown open, halogen lamps knocked over, and sofas turned upside down. A mountain of books lay strewn on the floor. Sam ran to the front door, which was ajar, and saw that the lock had been smashed. A burglary! Someone had broken in! It could have been anyone looking for money or valuables — Barenboim Street wasn't in the best of neighborhoods — but when it came to motive, there was only one likely suspect: the Arkeos man from the museum. But in that case . . . Sam felt a stab of fear rise from his stomach and shoot up his throat. The stone statue! What if the man was looking for the stone statue?

In a panic, he raced down to the basement, rushed across the room, lifted the heavy unicorn tapestry, and burst into the secret storeroom. He grabbed the night-light and switched it on. Whew! The stone was still there, perfectly intact. Apparently nobody had been in the secret room. But then what could the burglar have been searching for?

Sam went back upstairs, feeling puzzled. Everything had been turned upside down and carefully searched: drawers yanked open, cushions uncovered, and carpets lifted. One of the tear-gas canisters his father had bought to protect the store had rolled under a radiator. But what seemed to have interested the intruder most were the books. All the shelves were empty. Several books had their covers ripped off; some were stacked, others scattered, and most had wound up in a pile in the middle of the reading room. It was impossible to tell if any works had been stolen, and if so, how many.

Sam dropped into the only armchair still upright and stared at the disaster. What was the Arkeos man after? Information about Allan? The Book of Time? The black notebook? At that thought, Sam congratulated himself for having put both back in their hiding place, fiercely guarded by the vicious Zan. There, at least, they were safe.

The question now was what to do about all this. He'd come to the bookstore that morning planning to go into Time again to continue his quest for two more coins. If he called Grandma now, she would notify the police, which would mean he wouldn't have access to the stone statue until much later. But if Sam didn't do anything, the store would remain unlocked and unguarded, and the Arkeos man could come back again at his leisure.

He spent a moment weighing the pros and cons. Two measly little coins! That meant just a few round trips in Time, which wouldn't take more than a few hours in the present. Besides, it wasn't likely that the Arkeos man would dare to show up at the bookstore in broad daylight. If Sam was lucky, he might be able to get all seven coins by that evening. Then he could take care of the things he had to do: tell Grandma, call the police, and so on.

Once Sam made his decision, he wedged a chair against the front door and changed into his stylish "time traveler" outfit from the Chez Faulkner fashion house. Then he went down to the basement and knelt beside the stone statue. He put two coins in the cavity — the museum coin and the Delphi coin — and placed the third, the one with Arabic writing, in the center of the sun. He waited for a few moments for the faint humming to begin. But just as he put his hand on the rough, rounded top, he heard steps in the basement.

"Sam?" someone called.

He tried to lift his fingers off the stone, but a magnetic force seemed to hold them fast.

"Sammy? It's me, Lily."

Those last words were accompanied by the sound of the tapestry being lifted and the door opening.

"Sam, wait! No! The police are coming. They —"

Sam's arm was starting to burn more and more. He braced himself, straining with all his might not to be carried away, but molten fire was flowing irresistibly up his veins.

"No! You have to . . ."

He felt Lily's cool hand on his burning shoulder, but it wasn't enough. He was already being sucked into space.

*   *   *

Sam landed heavily, with something even heavier pressing against his back. Resisting the urge to throw up, he struggled to free himself from the burden. Then he realized that the thing in question was a body huddled against him, and it was weeping and gagging.

"Illil?" The syllables sounded garbled and unintelligible in his mouth. His cousin rolled onto her side, moaning, then turned away and vomited. In the darkness Sam could see her only as a light shape crouched on the cold, damp soil. What was Lily doing there? By what miracle had she followed him? He looked around for the stone. It was less than a yard away, topped with a skull and scraps of animal skins. A little farther on, he could see a tiny flame rising from a crude dish. Sam suspected what had happened and had a bad feeling about it.

"Ahhhrrg!"

Lily staggered to her feet. She was wearing the same kind of nightgown that Sam wore on his very first time-travel trip, to the island of Iona.

"Ilil! Ata?" he asked. That wasn't exactly what he meant to say, but it was all that came out.

She turned to him in tears. "Ammy! Ata na?" Her face was twisted by pain and overwhelming panic.

"Ilil, mon na!" said Sam, trying to calm her.

It was difficult to talk, as this language didn't seem to have all the words he wanted to say, resulting in a series of guttural grunts. And of course Lily had never experienced the strangeness of the automatic translator before. . . . He took her in his arms and hugged her tight.

"Ammy!" she wailed. "Ammy!"

When she had calmed down a little, she tugged at his sleeve and pointed forcefully at the stone statue. But Sam had no intention of leaving right away, regardless of the seriousness of their new situation. Each jump through time cost him a coin, and leaving without picking up a few extras was out of the question. Besides, if Lily was no longer in the present to help him get back, how would they make the trip home? It was best to think things over before they took any steps.

Sam pulled his cousin gently but firmly toward the crude lamp. Flickering in the slight draft, the flame made shadows on the rocky wall.

"Ngol?" asked Lily.

"Ngol," Sam agreed. It was the only word that came up to express the idea of a cave. Even so, it didn't mean "cave" exactly, but rather "shelter from the winds where we are together" — more or less.

It was then that the cave suddenly seemed to come to life before their eyes. A kind of bull or bison outlined in black floated on the stone, heaving in the shifting light; then a big horse with dots on its body, and another, smaller bison facing them. In all, there were a half-dozen animals painted on the rock wall!

"Langda!" exclaimed Sam, which apparently meant "spirit of creatures that dance on the rock."

He was both fascinated and frightened. The stone had clearly taken them on a gigantic leap into the past. Were they in prehistoric times? Their primitive language seemed to confirm it. Despite his anxiety, Sam felt strangely elated. They'd studied prehistoric art in school, and he had often daydreamed over reproductions of these very same fifteen- or twenty-thousand-year-old paintings. He carefully picked up the grease lamp and held it next to the wall. A herd of deer burst out of nowhere, as if fleeing a predator's attack. Sam and Lily had the first masterpieces of human history under their very eyes!

"Na!" said Lily, pointing at something.

Sam came closer. A nearly perfect red circle had been painted between one pair of antlers, as if the sun were rising behind the deer. Was this a rough draft of the strange U that had inspired Arkeos? *Of course not!* Sam told himself firmly. It could only be a coincidence; it was a vague resemblance at best.

He set down the dish and took Lily's hand to lead her toward what appeared to be the exit: a sloping passageway that rose about twenty yards to another large, dimly lit room.

"Mingo, Ammy, mingo!"

She was right. After making their way around various obstacles — rockfalls and stalagmites — they reached the cave entrance. It was on the edge of a rocky cliff above a river. The air was cool, the weather overcast, and the surroundings looked both wild and familiar: big trees, rushing water, stone outcroppings, and in the distance, grassy mountains. For a moment, Sam almost expected to see the long neck of a brontosaurus or the toothy jaws of a Baryonyx appear between the trees. But of course (with apologies to *The Flintstones*), tens of millions of years separated dinosaurs and prehistoric people — which was just as well!

The only path went upward, so Sam and Lily climbed the hill, stopping often to check for movement and sound: birdsong, a distant growling, a rabbit hopping through the bushes.

That's when they saw it, its powerful brown head rising above some boulders barely a hundred yards away. Nose in the wind, it was sniffing for scents — sniffing *their* scent.

"Igba! Igba!" screamed Lily.

There was no gap in the vocabulary here. It was a bear, a huge bear!

"Ngol!" Sam ordered.

They ran back the way they'd come as fast as they could, bruising their feet on the rough ground. Behind them, the bear growled so loudly that the birds fell silent or flew away. Then it took off after them with surprising agility, its growls filling the air like thunder.

"Nita, Ilil, nita!" Sam urged.

By the time they reached the cave, the bear was only twenty yards behind them. Luckily, its weight caused a rockfall and it lost its balance.

"Grrroarr!" roared the bear.

Lily and Sam rushed into the cave, still hand in hand. Sam dragged her toward what he guessed was the passage leading to the stone statue, hoping the bear would be too bulky to follow them. Bursting into the dimly lit space, he picked up the lamp and searched for a place to hide. The cave's ceiling was rough and its walls laced with cracks, but none were big enough to take shelter in. They could have tried to use the stone statue, but Sam knew from experience that it could take a full minute before it worked — much too long. And what if Lily got accidentally left behind, maybe forever? The bear roared in the distance, its growls multiplied by the echoes in the cave.

"Ammy!" Lily was pointing up at something. Flowing water had carved a kind of natural chimney at the back of the chamber. Sam ran over to it. The vertical crack was about a foot and a half wide. If he gave Lily a leg up, she could probably climb into it. And then by using his arms . . .

"Ilil! Nita!"

She put her foot on the step he made with his locked fingers. She put her other foot on his shoulder, and Sam had to lean against the rock to remain upright under her weight.

The bear was no longer growling, but in its place they could hear an ominous snuffling: It was tracking them. A rubbing noise on the rock revealed it had found the passageway and was getting close.

"Nita, Ilil!" whispered Sam, grimacing.

The burden on his shoulders lifted at the very moment that the bear burst in. It was gigantic, at least ten feet tall, with nightmare claws and evil little eyes that glittered in the darkness. It reared up on its hind legs with a growl of triumph, clawing at the wall. "Nita, Ammy," Lily whispered to him.

But Sam felt paralyzed by fear. Confident that its prey couldn't escape, the bear came a few yards closer, shambling along like a big, harmless teddy bear — except it wasn't coming for a playdate. In desperation, Sam waved his ridiculous lamp, but the bear seemed unimpressed by the tiny flame. The pathetic flicker cast a light on the stone statue adorned with the bones and animal skins; and for some inexplicable reason, the sight enraged the bear.

"Grrouammmarrrr!" it roared.

The bear threw its full weight at the stone, pounding it with huge paws until the rock shook. *Blam! Blam!* Chips flew into the air as the bear attacked the stone. *It was going to destroy the stone statue!*

81

Sam finally snapped out of his daze.

"Nounka igba," he screamed with desperate rage, trying to get its attention. "Nounka, nounka!"

The animal suddenly seemed to remember him, though that didn't improve its vicious mood. It bounded smoothly over to Sam and gave him one last look before pulling back for the blow that would rip his head off.

"Nangada igba gonka!" yelled a powerful voice behind it.

The animal spun around, and Sam had the time to glimpse a hairy man armed with a spear, who was about to heave it at the bear. Then the rocky ceiling seemed to collapse on his head and everything went black.

"Igba na katam," someone said.

Sam opened his eyes. It was almost night. He was lying on the ground with an animal skin pulled up to his chin. A bright fire was burning at the entrance to a nearby cave, with figures gathered around it. The fashion here definitely ran to hair growing out of every possible place: foreheads, ears, legs, arms . . . Chewbacca and family!

"Igba noom noom!" said the one who was speaking to the group.

The others agreed with little clicks of their tongues, and as Sam's head cleared, he made an effort to understand what they were saying. The internal translation was wordy but effective.

"I was collecting stones-with-colors to give blood and fur to the animals-that-dance-on-the rock," said the speaker. "Then the big-male-standing-up growled and growled — *igba noom noom*. It came from the cave-where-animal-spirits-hide, up the hill," he added, displaying a gift for suspense.

Under the animal skin, Sam could feel that his arms and legs were tied. He was a prisoner. Very slowly he raised himself on one elbow to see if he could find his cousin. There were about fifteen people around the fire, men and women, but none resembled Lily — or ever would, even after a head-to-toe waxing. What had happened to her? Had she also been caught or had she managed to escape? Did she think he was dead? Assuming the stone statue was still standing, had she used it to go home?

"I took the stick-that-stabs," continued the speaker, "and went to see if the magic of the drawings had breathed life into the creatures-who-dance. The great igba was there, in the Cave of Spirits. He was hitting the Mother-stone with all his strength!"

Hearing of the Mother-stone's misfortune produced angry tongue clicks. As Sam's eyes gradually adapted to the darkness, he was able to make out the bear's skin, stretched over a frame of branches a few yards away. The animal had been cut into quarters. Pieces of meat were hanging under the shelter of the cave. So that's where the stench was coming from!

"Igba had torn the skins from the Mother-stone. Igba wanted the Mother-stone to be cold, so the drawing magic would not work!"

The clan seemed to agree with this interpretation and showed its discontent by waving its fists at igba, who was in no shape to respond.

"The stick-that-stabs went deep into igba's stomach. He growled and growled — *igba noom noom*. Then the big-male-standing-up fell backward, and I saw the little-white-fur-man."

At once, all eyes turned to Sam, who barely had time to close his eyes and pretend to be asleep.

"Bring him, Sharp-teeth," ordered the speaker.

A moment later Sam felt himself being lifted and his bonds untied. He pretended to have trouble awakening, and the tongue clicks turned quizzical. Sharp-teeth carried him effortlessly over to the clan group and sat him down near the fire. The others came closer to touch him. Stinking of grease, they inspected him every which way, fiddling with his hair, pinching his skin — they were surprised at how smooth it was — parting his lips to feel his tongue, and spreading his toes, amazed that he could walk on such small feet. All this was done with exclamations of surprise and occasionally disgust. It was as scary as *The Night of the Living Dead,* and Sam had to struggle not to shudder at the stroking or the smell.

After a few moments, the speaker ended the introductions and spoke to him. "Where do you come from, little-white-fur-man?"

Sam chose to keep quiet. He was afraid that if he couldn't give a believable explanation, he might irritate these guys, all of whom were a full head taller and at least a hundred pounds heavier than he was.

"He can't talk," concluded a woman. Her extraordinarily hairy mass reminded Sam of Mrs. Pinson, his music teacher, after a major blow-dry failure.

"He can't run either," added her neighbor, pointing to Sam's feet.

"He could never hunt a long-nose with such skinny arms," said a bearded man with a scarred cheek.

"He isn't like us," added prehistory's version of Mrs. Pinson. "Is he a two-legged screamer that has lost its fur?"

"Two-legged screamers have long tails," the speaker objected, "and they don't often come close to the shelters-from-the-wind. The little-white-fur-man was in the Cave of Spirits when igba fell on him."

So that was it, thought Sam. He'd been knocked out by the weight of the falling bear!

An old man who hadn't spoken until then stood up and leaned on a crudely carved staff.

"The clan must be careful," he croaked. "Remember the words of He-who-comes-from-far! All those not of the clan who approach the Mother-stone must be killed! All of them!" He took two steps toward Sam and waved his staff under his nose. "They must be killed or the hunt will be bad, the streams will dry up, and the clan will have nothing to eat! That is what He-who-comes-from-far said. That is what the clan must do!"

Sam couldn't decide which was the most frightening: the old man's ruined, scarred eye socket, the stench of his breath, or the decoration on top of his stick — a black bone shaped like a pair of horns with a round shell stuck between them. It was exactly like the strange U on the picture of the deer in the cave — the Arkeos symbol!

The speaker objected, saying, "Come, Death-eye, I was only a child when He-who-comes-from-far visited our clan. He never came back, and many of our fathers said he was dangerous."

"Yes, he was dangerous, but he had power," yelled the old man. "He could kill Sharp-teeth with a single glance, and the entire clan along with him! That is why we must obey him and kill all those who approach the Mother-stone. Or else he will return and kill us!"

Just as Sam started thinking it might be time for him to say something, a high-pitched scream rang out: "ANIANIIIII!" The livelier ones seized their spears, but Death-eye grabbed Sam by the neck to keep him from moving.

"IGBA ANIANIIIII!"

"There, above the cave!" said the prehistoric Pinson, pointing.

"The child-of-the-bear!" screamed the voice. "Release the child-of-the-bear!"

A horned demon had suddenly appeared a few yards above the flames, standing on top of the mouth of the cave, one foot extended into empty space. It had a bleached bear skull for a head, scraps of fur for its skin, and blood running down its arms. The orange glow from the fire combined with the pale moonlight to give the hideous creature an unearthly aura. The brave hunter aimed his spear, but the speaker stopped him as the demon screamed again: "Lightning and fire on the clan if you don't give up the child-of-the-bear!"

The frightened members of the tribe backed away, a few of them covering their ears or eyes. Even the hunter no longer seemed quite so eager to confront the horrible sight. Sam, however, welcomed the intrusion. Decked out in the skull and animal skins that covered the Mother-stone, Lily had come to rescue him!

"Let him go, Death-eye!" the speaker ordered.

The man did so regretfully, and Sam raced up to the cave mouth.

Lily went on threatening the frightened group huddled at her feet. "Lightning and fire on whoever dares disturb the spirit of the big-male-standing-up!" she intoned.

The warning must have hit home, because she and Sam took off running without anyone making a move to follow.

"Hurry!" urged Lily, pointing Sam up the hill.

Without turning around they ran to the spirit cave several hundred yards away and into its murky depths. It was only when they reached the stone statue that his cousin took off the furs and skull and carefully placed them next to the lamp. Her red-spattered gown looked as if it had been dipped in the bear's blood. She took one of the two coins from the cavity and thrust it at him.

"Quick, Sammy!"

Though reluctant to use up one of his five coins, Sam realized they didn't have any choice. As he slapped the ram's head on the sun, he observed the great claw marks and fragments left by the bear. The animal had clearly tried to destroy the stone statue, but why?

When Sam judged the humming was strong enough, he gripped his cousin by the waist and held her as tightly as he could. Only then did he put his hand on the stone's rounded top.

CHAPTER TEN

Slaves!

With a loud thump, the two of them rolled against something hard. Lily remained hunched over with nausea for a moment while Sam tried to orient himself. They were in a dark, low-ceilinged room with wooden machinery of some sort on the left and a rectangular porthole set in the wall. Sam stood up and put his eye to the scratched, blurry glass. The next room contained a huge vat of water and a waterwheel, which wasn't turning at the moment. In their room, some mallets and tongs lay on the ground a little distance away, along with an oil lamp of a model distinctly more evolved than the one in the spirit cave. The stone statue stood against the opposite wall, but covered with such a thick layer of saltpeter that the carved sun was barely visible. Dampness oozed down the walls, and everything felt wet.

Sam retrieved the museum coin from the stone's cavity and bent over his cousin.

"Are you okay, Lily?"

"The skull," she muttered, wiping her mouth.

"It's over. We did it!"

"Did what?"

"We escaped."

"Have you taken up Latin, Sammy?"

"What?"

"You're speaking Latin — and so am I."

"Oh!"

"Terrific, this instant translation thing," she added with a weak smile. "If only I had it with my teacher . . ."

She fell silent and listened. Muffled voices could be heard from the underground area stretching off into the darkness, voices that seemed to be coming closer.

"There's something I have to tell you, Sam. It's about our present."

"I'm listening."

"The police are looking for you."

"The police?"

"Yes, because of the burglary at the Sainte-Mary Museum. They found your cell phone in the room where the theft happened."

His cell! He'd completely forgotten about it!

"They checked the numbers and showed up at Grandma's around noon. You'd already left, and they said they were going to Barenboim Street to find you. Mom and I had just come back from the water park and I rushed over to warn you. But when I tried to catch you —" She looked around at the ancient machinery.

"When they find out the bookstore has been robbed too, there's going to be fireworks," Sam said.

"So that's why all those books were on the floor!"

"It was probably the Arkeos man — the guy with the tattoo," Sam explained. "I think he's looking for something, the black notebook, maybe, or the Book of Time. On the Internet I found this company called Arkeos that sells antiquities —"

"Shhh!" hissed Lily. "They're coming!"

The conversation from the underground was becoming clearer.

"It's the oldest part of the complex, Corvus. We really ought to think about closing it. The leaks are getting worse and —"

"What are you talking about?" thundered a second voice. "It's the middle of summer, and we're swamped with customers! I need all of our facilities at full power! I want you to fix it, and fast!"

"They're nearly here," whispered Lily. "What should we do?"

Sam had her stand up and brush herself off. A yellowish glow appeared in the underground hallway, getting ever brighter.

"I'm not going to let some little leak keep me from opening, Julius. And I don't pay you to tell me that you can't set things right. What do I . . ."

The two men entered the machinery room. Seeing Sam and Lily, they stopped dead.

"*What are you doing here?*" screamed the one who was holding the lamp, a chubby bald man wearing a toga.

"We got lost —" Sam began.

"Since when do slaves have the right to wander around underground? And where's your uniform?"

"Er . . . I forgot it," Sam said.

90

"What you mean, you forgot it?" He raised the stick in his right hand and gave Sam a sharp crack on the legs. "The baths are about to open and you aren't at your stations? What are your names?"

Lily was quicker than her cousin. "Samus and Lilia," she answered.

"That doesn't ring a bell," said the bald man, waving his stick. "Did Petrus buy you for the end of the season?"

"Yes, it was Petrus," she said coolly.

"Well, I hope you didn't cost me too much, you filthy little lazybones. One really can't find a slave worthy of the name anymore! All right, Julius, I'll give you half an hour to get the waterwheel working again. As for you two —" He gave Sam another blow with the stick. "Go to your work, and hop to it!"

Still spewing abuse, Corvus marched them through the underground passage to a stone stairway leading to the open air.

"My God," whispered Lily as they emerged.

They were in a huge rectangular quad bordered by columned galleries and stone buildings. Trimmed green grass grew in the open central area. In the distance, a mountain with a few planted fields on its lower slopes loomed above the rooftops. The sun wasn't high yet, but it was already pleasantly warm. Servants in simple tunics bustled about, their arms loaded with towels, fruit, and amphoras. Corvus directed Sam and Lily to a room on the right.

"Hustle over to the laundry to change, then go to your stations right away. Petrus should be here any minute. Until then, I'll have my eye on you, believe me!"

91

He waved the stick over his head for emphasis, and they had no choice but to obey.

"What you think we should do?" asked Lily quietly as they walked toward the laundry.

"We've absolutely got to find some coins," answered Sam, also quietly. "The stone statue works, so that means there's at least one coin somewhere nearby. Where do you think we are?"

"At a Roman bath. They're like public swimming pools, and they were all over the Roman Empire. People would go there to get clean and do business."

A cheerful-looking matron greeted them with a broad smile. "So, children, are you new here?"

"Yes, ma'am," said Sam. "Petrus just bought us."

"So much the better, we're shorthanded these days. You'll be needing something clean to wear, I suppose?"

She took two tunics from the piles lining the walls and held them out to the children.

"These should fit you all right. But you'd better hurry, we'll be opening soon. Were you told what you were supposed to do?"

"Not yet."

"Ah! And of course that lazy slug Petrus isn't here yet!" To Lily, she said, "Go to the women's changing room at the end of the palaestra and ask for Alvina." To Sam: "As for you, the men's locker room is right next door. Old Trimalchion will fill you in."

They came out wearing their new uniforms, wondering what their next move should be.

"Suppose we left right away?" suggested Lily.

"No, we *have* to get more coins! Besides, the guy fixing the waterwheel must still be down there with the stone. Let's wait until he —"

Just then, a sharp crack echoed off the portico's marble panels. "By Jupiter!" screamed Corvus, rapping on the ground. "Are you still dillydallying around here? *Get to work!*"

If Sam had been asked what he planned to be when he grew up — two thousand years earlier, in this case — he would have answered unhesitatingly, "Anything except a slave in the Roman baths!" At first glance, it looked like a job that anybody could do, but it turned out to be exhausting in practice. Trimalchion, an old black slave with two missing fingers, explained the basics of the work, and Sam was quite literally tossed into the bathwater.

He was first assigned to the locker room, where the many clients came to change. He took their clothes, put them in lockers, and gave back towels in exchange — an easy job. But when Corvus passed by, he decided that a strapping young fellow like Sam should be employed doing something more energetic. So Corvus sent him to the caldarium, or hot room, a kind of early sauna. Sam's job was to keep the very hot pool of water clean by scrubbing it with a rough mop. As he scoured the basin, Sam realized that the mosaic on the bottom showed a beautiful white lyre held by a half-naked couple. There was nothing astonishing about that, *except that the instrument was shaped like two horns containing a circle!* Here was the Arkeos symbol at the bottom of a pool in the Roman Empire!

Shaken by his discovery, Sam put down his mop and went to question Trimalchion.

"Excuse me, but do you know who designed the mosaic in the pool?"

"You mean the man and the woman with the lyre? It was redone a few years ago by a local man named Octavius. Why? Is there a broken tile?"

"No, I just think it's beautiful. Are there any others like it in the baths?"

Trimalchion thought for a moment. "Mosaics like that, no. It must be the only one. Now that I think of it, I think the idea actually came from one of Octavius's workers — a peculiar fellow who just disappeared one day without collecting his pay. But the design was already laid out and the master of the baths seemed to like it, so . . . That kind of lyre is supposed to bring happiness and prosperity — not that I'd know anything about that!" Then he added quietly: "You better get back to work. Here comes Corvus."

Realizing that Sam had abandoned his post, Corvus first threatened him with his stick, then as punishment gave him a job that Sam couldn't have imagined in his worst nightmares. For half an hour he walked around the palaestra carrying a pot, and men relieved themselves into it between wrestling or bowling matches. Sam then had to dump the urine into a large vat off to one side, where laundry workers used its contents to wash clothes. Washing clothes in urine — frankly, it was enough to make you puke.

Sam had become a traveling toilet.

After a while the temptation to explore became too strong, and he sneaked off to the stairway that led underground. The wooden wheel was turning again and squeaking like an old door, drawing water up from the vat and filling a tank that in turn supplied the baths. The fact that the wheel was turning must mean that the worker responsible for fixing it had finished his job.

But when Sam reached the bottom of the staircase, he made a painful discovery: A locked and rusty gate barred the way underground. He couldn't get to the stone statue!

"You again!" screamed Corvus when he saw Sam emerge. "What are you doing, snooping around down there?"

This time, he hit Sam twice across the back and sent him directly to the furnace room on the lower level, reputedly the worst place in the baths. There Sam met two gigantic black slaves, their skin gleaming with sweat, who were heaving logs onto big fires. Above the fires, huge cauldrons filled with boiling water produced the steam that heated the caldarium, carried there by a system of ducts. The furnace room itself was as hot as seven devils.

"Work him until he drops!" Corvus instructed the two slaves. "This boy needs to learn who his master is!"

The two men stepped aside for a moment to let Sam pick up his first log, but as soon as Corvus's back was turned, they took it out of his hands.

"The old crow doesn't know what he's thinking anymore," sighed one, mopping his brow. "You won't last long in this inferno. Go sit over there instead."

Delighted by his good luck, Sam was about to sit on a twisted stool when the ground suddenly began to shake underfoot. Without quite knowing how it happened, he found himself sprawled on his back.

The two slaves burst out laughing. "Hah! You didn't expect that, did you, boy? Sometimes the earth gets angry around here. You have to know how to stay on your feet!"

But at the very next moment, an even stronger tremor sent them crashing into each other. White dust poured down from the ceiling and several burning logs rolled out of the fire. Water sloshed furiously against the edges of the huge vat.

"Well, that was something!" said the taller of the two as he straightened up. "That time, it really moved!"

"If it happens again, maybe we better put the furnace out to avoid a fire," remarked the other one. "When this kind of thing starts . . ."

They checked for damage to the furnace, then went up to get their orders from Corvus. Sam followed. At the bathers' level, people seemed alarmed. Towels wrapped around their waists, they were pouring out of the buildings to see what was happening. Statues had toppled over and a few tiles had fallen from the roofs, but the matter of greatest concern was a very deep, dull rumbling. A few dozen customers had gathered in the middle of the palaestra to point at something in the distance: a wisp of black smoke rising from the top of the mountain.

Sam was startled when a cool hand slipped into his. It was Lily, whom he hadn't heard coming.

"Sam! I've been looking for you for the last quarter of an hour, and I've got bad news. Do you know the name of that mountain?

"No."

"It's Vesuvius, the volcano! We're in Pompeii, Sammy — Pompeii!"

96

CHAPTER ELEVEN

August 4, 79 A.D., Ten A.M.

"It's on fire!" a woman screamed. "The mountain's on fire!" Bathers and slaves gathered around her, looking frightened.

Corvus tried to reassure them. "No, no, that's just a big dark cloud on the mountaintop. Come back to the baths, Citizen Flavia, there's nothing to fear."

"Nothing to fear?" asked a man who had been playing ball in the palaestra. "This tile nearly knocked me out!" He brandished the tile as if Corvus himself had thrown it.

"We know there have been tremors these last few days, Marius, but they're not dangerous. Our establishment is well designed and —"

"What about the earthquake seventeen years ago?" snapped another man. "Wasn't that dangerous? Half the city was destroyed, and the Stabian Baths were badly damaged, as I recall."

At those words, large beads of sweat appeared on Corvus's bald head.

"That was different," he said, sounding embarrassed. "We've reinforced the walls since then, and strengthened the pools."

He switched to a falsely playful tone. "Come, my friends. A cup of our best wine to the first people who go back to the caldarium — on the house!" To the slaves, he snapped: "And you, get back to work and take care of our guests!"

A murmur of uncertainty went through the customers. The sun was getting hot and the sky was a limpid blue; it looked like the start of a beautiful day. There was that unusual smoke, of course, but how could a catastrophe ever happen in such fine weather?

Then Lily ran to the center of the group. "If you don't leave town right away," she said firmly, "you're all going to die!"

Fast as a striking snake, Corvus gave her a resounding slap. It sent Lily tumbling to the feet of the woman called Flavia. "You filthy little liar!" he screamed. "I promise, you're going to —"

But the threat was quickly drowned out by an enormous explosion: *GGRRRBBBRRRAAAOUMMMM!* With unimaginable power, the top of Mount Vesuvius blew off, shooting gigantic chunks of rock into the air. There was a moment of astonishment as they watched extraordinary whistling fireballs cut across the sky and land in the distance.

"The mountain is spilling its guts!"

"The girl's right, we're all going to die!"

"Wait, friends! Vesuvius is far away! Enjoy the spectacle," Corvus urged them. "You can return to the baths afterward."

But most of the visitors were in no mood for relaxation.

"Open the locker rooms, Corvus! We want our clothes!"

"Yes, our clothes!" chorused several voices.

"In that case . . ." he said with resignation. Corvus gave the key ring to old Trimalchion, whom most of the bathers followed to retrieve their things.

One of the slaves who had been stoking the furnace spoke up. "Corvus, if the earth continues to rage, you should let us go to our families."

"What?" shouted the master of the baths, his scalp turning purple. "Since when do slaves decide what they should or shouldn't do?"

"If we stay here, we will all die!" Lily repeated. "Pompeii will be buried in ash!"

"As for you," screamed Corvus, "if you say another word, I'll knock your head off with this stick. Ashes? That's nonsense! Vesuvius is not a fire mountain, everyone knows that! I want all you slaves back to your jobs immediately. Nobody leaves the establishment before nightfall!"

The furnace stoker spoke up again, louder this time. "Corvus, this girl may be right. The ground is shaking and the mountain is on fire. You have to let us leave! Remember what happened to my daughter!"

Corvus's stick hissed through the air and hit the stoker's cheek with a terrible crack. It opened a crimson cut that began to bleed.

"Xenon, Flactus, Trilcien!" Corvus called. "Take Diomedes and lock him up in the warm room, the one with the deadbolt. There are ten sestertia in it for you! And while you're at it, take care of this bird of ill omen!" He caught Lily by the elbow and shoved her into the arms of a huge man with thinning red hair. Sam ran to intervene but was soon seized in turn, as the promise of sestertia energized the other servants.

"Lock the boy up too! That one's done nothing but get on my nerves all morning!"

"It's hailing!" said the laundress in wonder. "Imagine, hail out of a clear blue sky!"

As Sam struggled to free himself from the powerful hands of the tall, thin man restraining him, he felt something bounce off his neck.

"That isn't hail, those are stones!" someone called.

Stones were falling in volleys — some large, some small, but most about the size of an egg. They were rough, irregular, and gray, but curiously quite light.

"Look, it's the mountain! It's spewing stones!"

Indeed, a dark plume had formed over Vesuvius that grew thicker as it drifted toward the city.

"Xenon, lock those three up," ordered Corvus. "And you others, start picking up the stones. I want the palaestra to be clean as a whistle when this is over."

Diomedes, Sam, and Lily were hustled to the women's baths and thrown into the tepidarium, the warm room. The stones pelting the roof made a deafening racket, but the sound didn't keep Diomedes from yelling as he threw himself against the door: "Corvus, damn you! I have to find my wife and daughter! They need me! If anything happens to them . . ."

Lily took Sam aside. "Those stones falling from the sky are pumice, Sam! We saw a documentary about it at school — it's a sign that the eruption has really started. In a few hours, the town will be completely buried in ash!"

"A few hours — are you sure?"

"Maybe less, I don't know. What I do know is that a lot of people died in Pompeii — men, women, children, everyone.

This burning cloud came out of the mountain, and they were all mummified by the ash. People were found centuries later in the exact position they were in at the moment they died!"

"You have any other good news?"

"We have to get out of here, Sammy, and fast!"

Sam quickly scanned the interior of the warm room. It had some high windows, but he couldn't reach them, even standing on Diomedes's shoulders. Nor was there much else of use: amphoras of oil, scrapers for bathers' skin, two discarded towels, a poker to stir the fire, and a few oil lamps burning by the pool. Colored frescoes illustrating the pleasures of the baths decorated the walls, but there was no emergency exit to be seen.

"A plague on that Corvus," raged Diomedes, turning toward them. "May his teeth fall out into his mouth and choke him! My daughter is too weak to walk, and my wife will never be able to carry her. And it's all his fault!"

"Did he hurt your daughter?" asked Lily.

"He made her go up on a balcony to hang flowers, and she fell. She was much too young for the job! Since then, her legs won't hold her anymore. And if what you say is true, if the mountain is spitting fire . . ." He took Lily's hands in his and squatted down to her level. "You're almost the same age as my daughter, yet you seem so sure of yourself! Do you really think we're going to die?"

"Well, there's always hope, isn't there?" Lily murmured, gently freeing herself. "But Vesuvius seems to have come to life, and —"

A brutal tremor rocked the walls then, and the floor heaved. The three prisoners staggered for a moment as the building groaned. A frightening creaking could be heard outside, as if the structure next door had fallen.

"What was that?" asked Lily.

"It came from the south corner," said Diomedes. "I hope the big water tower didn't collapse."

"Is there a way to get out of here?" Sam asked insistently.

"Besides this door, no. Unless . . ." The furnace stoker stepped back a few feet and pointed at the floor. "Look, the tiles cracked. With a little bit of luck . . . Bring me that poker, quick!"

Sam ran to get the iron rod near the fire. "You have an idea?"

"If we're able to widen this crack . . ."

He broke a few more tiles, then began enlarging the crack with the point of the poker. Outside, the shower of pumice stones fell heavier than ever. The light was fading, as if night were coming on.

"Grab the scrapers," said Diomedes, "and help me!"

Sam and Lily went to work with a will, scratching at the grainy cement that formed the room's foundation.

"Are you planning to dig a tunnel out?" asked Sam after a quarter hour of silent effort.

"You're close! The tepidarium and caldarium are raised above ground level. They rest on little columns, and hot air from the furnace circulates between them. That's how the rooms are kept at the right temperature. If we can get into the space between those columns . . . There! We've reached the brick layer. We're almost through!"

He made them stand back, gave a couple of mighty whacks with the poker, and broke through the final layer. Warm steam that smelled of dirt rose through the opening and made them cough.

"Isn't it dangerous down there?"

"The fire in the furnace is out. You two won't be in much danger."

"We two?"

"Yes, you. You're thin, and you should be able to squeeze through. I'm too big, and I'd get stuck. Come on, the hole isn't nearly big enough. Let's get to work!"

It took them another ten minutes to widen the crack enough for Sam and Lily to have a chance of squeezing into it.

"I'll give you a lamp," said Diomedes. "Get down there now! Hurry!"

"What about you, Diomedes?" Lily protested. "What's going to happen to you?"

"Don't worry about me. They're sure to let me out sooner or later." He tried to smile, but Lily and Sam weren't fooled. Corvus had no intention of freeing him.

"Get going!" he encouraged them. "If you follow the wall on the left toward the door, you'll reach a cleaning hatch. It has a wooden cover over it — a good kick should do the trick. And if . . . if you happen to meet my wife and my daughter, tell them I love them."

"I'm . . . I'm sure they love you too," stammered Sam, touched by his sacrifice.

After a final good-bye, Sam stretched out next to the hole, slid his arms, head, and chest into it, and almost immediately felt hard earth under his fingernails. If he kept his head low, he could just move ahead on his elbows and knees.

"Samus, the lamp!" Diomedes handed the oil lamp down

into the hole. Sam nearly knocked it over when he reached for it.

"Your turn, girl! Don't be afraid, it won't take long. Just follow the left-hand wall!"

Sam squeezed down as best he could to make room for Lily. They ignored the shards of brick and cement tearing at their skin as they slowly inched forward.

"You okay?" whispered Sam.

"Yeah, except for the heat and the dark," said Lily.

"It's like a snail race inside a radiator!"

After a laborious progression, they finally spotted the little cleaning hatch. Sam turned his body around — bruising both his shoulder and his hip in the process — so his feet rested against the hatch cover. Hunching down even farther to get momentum, he kicked at it with his heels. Something on the other side yielded and the hatch swung open with a bang.

"Good job, Sam!"

He let his cousin have the honor of getting out first, then she helped him up.

"Whew! Feels a lot better here!"

"Where are we?"

"I don't know," said Sam, lifting his lamp. "But this hallway must lead somewhere."

They stumbled on a door to a narrow staircase that led outside.

"Look at that stuff falling! It's incredible!"

A veritable rain of gray stones was falling on the baths, making a dense layer some four to six inches thick on the ground. The dark plume from Vesuvius now covered the city, so it looked like the middle of winter. Rumbling and occasional flashes of glowing orange light came from the volcano. The sound of shouts reached Sam and Lily from the distance, including Corvus's dulcet tones: "Faster! Lazy bunch of . . ."

"The trick is not to be spotted," muttered Sam. "Hide your face if you can!"

At the top of the stairs they stepped out into the palaestra near the portico. There wasn't much chance of Corvus noticing them; he was busy at the other end of the field, yelling at his men to clean the outdoor swimming pool. In the half-light, it wouldn't be hard to get to the stone statue. And maybe even . . .

"Wait, this way!" said Sam as he grabbed Lily and dragged her back toward the women's baths.

"What are you —"

"Diomedes!"

They crossed the empty vestibule and ran toward the tepidarium, whose door now rang with the slave's pounding.

"Let me out! *Let me out!*"

"Diomedes, we're here!"

"Samus, you did it!"

Sam shoved at the door with all his might, but it barely budged: The hinges and bolt were too strong. He took three steps back and launched himself against it even harder, but the only resulting crack came from his shoulder.

"Sammy, stop!"

Lily was pointing at something on the opposite wall: a key hanging from a large nail. Here was the history of the world, summed up in the blink of an eye: Men use their muscles, women use their brains!

Sam grabbed the key and turned it in the lock. Soon they were all hugging each other.

"Thank you, children, thank you! As soon as I get my wife and my daughter, I'll take you to safety!"

"That's impossible. We have to get something over by the old waterwheel. We'll join you later."

"The old waterwheel? I wouldn't go there if I were you. That's the weakest part of the complex, and with all these tremors . . ."

"We know what we have to do," said Lily. "Go on, and don't bother about us. Your wife and your daughter must be very worried."

Diomedes seemed about to object, but chose instead to hug them one last time. "Thank you again. And good luck!"

They parted under the portico, and Sam handed Lily one of the towels he had picked up in the tepidarium. "Put this on your head, it'll protect you from the stones."

They hugged the walls, praying that some huge block of pumice wouldn't come crashing down and flatten them. The palaestra now looked like a pebble beach. Over by the pool, Corvus was still barking at his servants, but their ranks had thinned considerably. The air smelled unpleasantly of something like natural gas or chemicals, and Lily began to cough.

"Sulfur," she spat. "We have to hurry!"

"It isn't very far now!"

But an unpleasant surprise awaited them. The building in whose cellar they'd appeared that morning was now half collapsed, with the great wooden wheel partly buried, sunk in bricks and debris. Water had flooded everything, including the stairway leading underground. The place looked as if a paddle wheel steamboat had smashed into the north wing of the baths.

"The water tank must have burst," Sam groaned.

He got as close as he could to the rubble, a soupy mass of debris and pumice. The stone statue was somewhere down below all that, ten or twelve feet under water.

"We don't have any choice," he said. "I'm going down."

He walked over to a beam that was still upright, held on to the buckets of the wheel, and slowly let himself sink.

"Be careful," said Lily. "It doesn't look very sturdy."

Taking a deep breath, Sam lowered himself into the cold, dark water until he reached the debris covering the bottom. He groped his way toward where he thought the stone should be, but soon ran into a tangle of planks. He was able to move only a couple aside before he had to go back up for air. It took several round-trips before Sam was able to reach the stone statue itself, and when he touched it, his heart sank: The top of the stone was broken off and jagged, probably shattered by a falling beam.

"Well?" asked Lily when he surfaced again.

She had taken shelter behind what was left of the overhang, and was using one hand to filter the increasingly noxious vapors. The rain of pumice stones had eased, but the smoke plume now displayed worrisome purple streaks.

"The stone's damaged, Lily. The whole top is gone."

"The whole top? The sun too?"

"No, the sun's intact, except maybe for a ray or two."

"Do you think it'll still work?"

"It *has* to work! Hurry!"

As his cousin joined him in the water, Sam took the museum coin from the corner of his pocket. Would the stone really work underwater, especially with part of it gone? Sam didn't have the slightest idea, but he didn't intend to end up mummified in Pompeii, a morbid attraction for twenty-first-century tourists.

"Hold my hand and don't let go. It's not very deep. You just have to take a big breath. Ready?"

Lily filled her lungs and nodded. Sam put the coin in his mouth. Together they dove and reached the bottom without difficulty. But once they had gone under the wheel, the water began to bubble furiously, and the planks that Sam had shoved aside began to tumble onto them. The earth was shaking again, and now their retreat was cut off!

In the dark, with the water churning all around, Lily started to panic. Sam had to grab her as he fumbled along the wall for the stone statue. When his fingers found its jagged top, he located the sun and clapped the coin onto it. Lily was now struggling to get free — a small, frightened animal desperate for light and air. But that wasn't an option anymore.

Sam tightened his grip on her and put his hand on the rough stone surface. He was beginning to run out of breath too, especially because Lily was kicking him in the stomach, but he had to hold on. After what seemed like forever — yellow butterflies were starting to dance in front of his eyes — something under his hand finally began to stir. Was it the stone or a last, deadly tremor?

CHAPTER TWELVE

Bulldozer

The whole world was shaking and full of incredible noise: *Ka-blam! Ka-blam!* Sam staggered to his feet, spitting out the dust that filled his mouth. Instead of water, he and Lily were submerged in a cloud of flying dirt that was only slightly easier to breathe.

"Lily?"

Sam's eyes stung, and he was having trouble keeping them open. It was almost completely dark, anyway.

"Lily?"

Ka-blam! Ka-blam! Were they still in Pompeii? Had they fallen into an air pocket somewhere while ashes blanketed the city above them?

"Here, Sammy," answered a faint, choked voice. "I'm over here."

"You're speaking English, Lily. Maybe —"

Ka-blam! Ka-blam!

"Are we in our basement?" Lily asked as she groped her way over to him. "What's going on?"

"I don't know, everything's shaking. Let's try and get out of here."

They heard something like the roar of an engine, and a section of ceiling came crashing down a few yards away.

"Excava —" Lily began.

Light streamed down through the opening, revealing iron steps leading upward on their left. The stairs ended a few feet from the ground. Sam lifted his cousin so she could climb out before the rest of the ceiling collapsed. *Rrrrmmm! Ka-blam! Ka-blam!*

Once upstairs, they hurried through a darkened room and emerged blinking in the open air. Around them were sections of ruined wall, a dangling broken window frame, smashed tiles, and —

"Look out!"

A mass of gleaming blue metal hurtled toward them. *Rrrrmmmm! Ka-blam! Ka-blam!* They threw themselves to one side as the blue monster jerked to a stop a yard away. It was a Caterpillar tractor with a huge metal blade in front.

"Good God almighty!" A man in a cap with a cigarette wedged in the corner of his mouth leaped down from the cab. "Good lord, kids! Where the heck do you think you are? This is a construction site! I could've crushed you!"

A couple of workers ran over to see what was happening.

"What's up, Ron?" shouted one. "Did you hit something?"

"It's these two kids, Jed. They just popped up in front of me. It was a near thing, I swear!"

Lily straightened up, brushed off her filthy, bloodstained tunic, and fixed her hair, as if she'd just stepped out of the bathroom. The man called Jed looked at the intruders with annoyance.

"This place is off-limits!" he shouted. "Didn't you see the signs? You're gonna get fined for this!"

Sam looked around. They were in an empty lot surrounded by fences and barbed wire. Old-fashioned earth-moving machines stood amid demolished houses and huge mounds of rubble. Beyond them rose dilapidated gray buildings, not the familiar hills of Sainte-Mary. They obviously weren't back on Barenboim Street! Yet there was a stone statue in the basement of the house, and these construction workers were about to destroy it.

"This belongs to us," said Sam angrily. "You don't have the right to tear it down!"

"We have every right, kid," answered Jed. "City permits and everything. If you lived here and your parents had to get out, that's not my fault. This is the Depression! So fork over the five-dollar fine or I'm handing you to the cops."

Five dollars, thought Sam, *but what kind of dollars? Canadian dollars, American dollars, Australian dollars?*

The bulldozer operator spoke up. "Don't be too hard on 'em, Jed. They're just kids. And you see what kind of shape they're in?"

"Listen, Ron, if hoboes start campin' in the work site, *we'll* be the ones that get fired, believe you me. That what you want?"

"Yeah, but we've got kids, right? What if it was them coming out of that hole?"

Jed shrugged. He didn't seem like a bad guy, just a foreman anxious to finish a job on time and avoid trouble. "Okay,

Ron, but get them the heck out of here. We've wasted enough time."

"You can't tear down that house!" protested Sam. "It's very valuable! There's something unique inside and . . ."

Ron grabbed Sam by the arm and yanked him close. "You listen to what we just told you, or you'll be hauled in for vagrancy on top of the fine. Your house is busted, can't ya see? Go try your luck somewheres else. You got your whole life ahead of you!"

Sam tried to resist, but the workmen were now in a hurry. They collared the children, frog-marched them to the exit, and sent them on their way. Jed kicked Sam in the rear for good measure.

"And if I catch you hangin' around here, I'm callin' the cops!"

Sam and Lily pretended to leave, but then they circled back to the fence, trying to find a way over it. Through a crack between two boards, they watched the bulldozer finish knocking down the remaining walls of the house, burying the stone under tons of debris.

"How are we ever going to get home?" asked Lily.

"I don't know," said Sam, a lump in his throat. "There must be some way." He swallowed. "It's not like we have any coins left anyway."

That realization made him feel worse than ever. Not only had he brought Lily with him into Time and nearly gotten her killed in three different eras, he now had no means of getting her home. They sat down on the ground, their backs against the fence, and he put his arm around his cousin. When he did, he realized that she was trembling despite the warm weather.

"Aren't you feeling well, Lily?" He rubbed her back and tickled her to cheer her up, but all he got was a weak smile.

"I'm scared, Sam."

He couldn't show her his own fear. "We'll pull through, Lily. We've always pulled through, haven't we? Look at the cave — the skull-and-furs trick was pure genius! And you were wonderful in Pompeii too, holding out underwater. You're a great time traveler and we're a terrific team, so we can't get discouraged now, okay? We'll find a way to get back home, I promise. First we've got to find some decent clothes. Then we'll wait for night and come back here, in case some piece of the statue survived. All right?"

Lily mumbled a vague yes, and Sam helped his cousin to her feet and looked around. On the left, there were one-story houses with neat grass pathways running between them; to the right, a row of shacks knocked together from scraps of wood and tin, with a dirt road on either side. There were other neighborhoods visible beyond that, and even a few skyscrapers in the distance. The city was very spread out and looked modern and unfinished at the same time. It wasn't a present-day city, but it wasn't the Wild West either. "The Depression," Jed had said, and that meant they were some time in the 1930s. Sam made up his mind when he saw laundry hanging on clotheslines behind the shanties on the right.

"What would you say to a nice new outfit, cousin? My treat."

They took the path farthest from the shacks, praying that people would be too busy to notice them. They saw three black children playing with a cat in one of the yards, but luckily they had their backs turned. About a hundred yards farther they came to what they were after: a large family's wash, with an array of mended shirts and shorts dangling from the clotheslines.

"I know what you're thinking," Sam whispered to Lily. "It isn't really a store, and we aren't going to pay for the clothes. But we don't have a choice!"

He jumped the low wooden fence and in two steps reached a shabby pair of blue canvas pants — an early version of blue jeans. Sam was usually pretty particular about his jeans; they had to be frayed to just the right degree, wide enough for comfort, and preferably with a low waist, so his underwear showed. But he didn't have a fashion show on his calendar that day, so he plucked off the clothespins and took the pants. He also grabbed a T-shirt that would suit his cousin, provided she liked her shirts very brown and very old. Then he noticed a shirt in his own size and stealthily moved to the end of the clothesline. But the white sheets and pillowcases lined up in front of him suddenly started to move.

"Who's that messing with my laundry?" A corner of a sheet lifted to reveal the face of an old black woman, who looked appalled. "Land sakes, you're robbing me, boy! Matthew! Come to the yard, quick! A little white boy is stealing your shirt!"

Sam leaped back and jumped over the fence without even realizing he'd done so.

"Matthew!" the woman called again. Sam grabbed his cousin by the arm and they took off running. "Matthew, your shirt's running away! You don't expect me to chase after it at my age, do you?"

"Thieves!" shouted another voice. "Thieves at Mama Lucy's!"

Several neighbors appeared at the window, and suddenly the yards were full of people. Two men rushed into the road to block their way, and children ran to catch up with them from behind.

"Thieves! They're robbing Mama Lucy!"

"All right, all right!" said Sam, stopping in his tracks. "We made a mistake. We're giving everything back!"

He waved the clothes as a sign of surrender, but that didn't keep a dozen people from surrounding him, yelling.

"They're the thieves from Mama Lucy's!"

"Let's call the police!"

"Nah, we'll take care of this ourselves! No mercy for thieves!"

"Besides, they ain't from around here!"

A sharp slap came from somewhere off to Sam's right, and his ear stung.

"Yeah! No need for police!"

Someone else punched Sam in the shoulder, and he turned to face his attacker. But then he saw the old woman from the clothesline, trotting toward the group and waving her arms.

"Have you gone crazy?" she yelled. "Leave them alone!"

"They're the ones, Mama Lucy. They stole your stuff!"

"Yeah, we'll show them!"

"You let that child go this instant, Bartholomew Jones," she said. "If your poor mother could see you now!"

The man who had grabbed Sam's wrist let it go and hung his head.

"Is this what they teach you in church on Sunday, boy?" she thundered. "Not to have compassion for the poorest among us?"

"They's in our neighborhood," protested Bartholomew. "If we ain't respected on our own ground . . ."

"Bartholomew Jones, you are some kind of fool! Remind me to box your ears next time I meet you! Have you seen their clothes? You really think they come from some fancy neighborhood for the pleasure of struttin' your rags?"

The man shrugged sheepishly.

"You two come along now," she told Sam and Lily. "I'll see what I can do for you."

The crowd parted, and Mama Lucy led the children to her house with the authority of a victorious general. Once there, she slammed her door in the face of any gawkers.

"You have to forgive them," she said. "Despair and misery makes them nasty! Everyone's out of work, especially here in the colored neighborhood. The kids are hungry, the parents don't know what to do. Lordy! But I don't need to tell you that, do I? You're so pale and skinny, little girl. . . ."

In fact, Lily's face looked waxen, and she had dark circles under her eyes.

"You want something to eat? Sit down, Mama Lucy must have some molasses cookies somewhere. And I'll fix you a nice cup of tea with sugar. That'll make you feel better. Matthew, are you there, big boy? You want some tea?"

Sam and Lily sat down on the faded armchairs, shaken by the turn of events and deeply ashamed at planning to steal from such a good woman. They were in a modest room filled with knickknacks, with a single window and a kerosene lamp that gave a cheerless light. The far wall was corrugated iron, partly covered by rows of old photos. There was also a treadle sewing machine, baskets overflowing with scraps of clothes, doilies on the furniture, a collection of colored bottles, and a half-open newspaper lying on a chair. Sam snatched it up and feverishly turned to the front page. "Presidential Election: Who Will the Democrats Pick?" Right above the headline was the paper's name and the date: *The Chicago Defender*, Thursday, June 30, 1932.

"Lily, we're in the United States," he whispered, "in Chicago in 1932. And look: The presidential elections are coming up!"

He handed her the newspaper, and Lily's eyes widened. "Chicago! In that case . . ."

"You kids interested in politics?"

A tall, slim young man had entered the room, elegant in a white uniform with gold buttons that seemed out of place in such humble surroundings. "Are you the ones everybody seems to be after? The dangerous criminals?"

"No, not criminals. It was a misunderstanding," said Sam defensively. "We lost our suitcases after a trip, and —"

At that point Mama Lucy came in, carrying a tray with steaming cups and a plate of cookies.

"Ah, you've met my Matthew! Handsome, isn't he? He's the pride of my old age! You off to work already, big boy? You don't want a little tea?"

Matthew took the newspaper from Lily. "I have to go to 91st Street," he said.

"Not more of that illegal betting, I hope? You know you could end up in the hoosegow for that."

"If I win, Mama Lucy, it sure helps make ends meet."

She shook her head. "What are you betting on this time?"

"The elections, of course! The candidate the Democrats will choose for the presidential election! It's in all the papers!"

"And how much do you hope to win on that?"

"For a fifty-dollar bet, as much as a thousand dollars! *If* I guess right."

"Roosevelt," muttered Lily wearily.

"Beg your pardon?"

"The Democrats will choose Roosevelt. His vice president will be John Garner."

Sam stared at her, bug-eyed. Roosevelt, all right; he'd heard of him. But that she should also know the American *vice* presidents . . .

"Roosevelt and Garner? I thought those two didn't get along!"

"Don't listen to her," Sam broke in with a forced chuckle. "My sister is a little out of it. Some days, she just says anything at all."

"Roosevelt and Garner," Matthew repeated thoughtfully. "Hmm . . . Well, why not?" He took his white cap from the coatrack and blew Mama Lucy a kiss as he went out the door. "See you tomorrow! I'll try not to get home too late."

The old lady looked after him adoringly. "What a boy! If you knew what shape he was in when I took him in! And now look at him!"

"You . . . you took him in?" said Sam, catching himself. He still couldn't believe the business about Roosevelt or his cousin's amazing store of historical trivia.

"Of course! Him and so many others! A dozen kids must have passed through my house. I've been a widow for twenty years, so what can I say? I don't have anything better to do

118

than give 'em a little love and comfort. Plus loads of laundry!"
She laughed at the thought. "Now there, I have done a few
loads of laundry! In fact, you should have come and *asked* me
for clothes instead of helping yourself. Mama Lucy always has
something for kids like you. You don't have any family anymore, I suppose?"

Lily answered first. "Not exactly. We have some relatives
here in Chicago. Have you ever heard of the Faulkner grocery
store?"

This time, Sam nearly choked on his cookie. The Faulkner
grocery store! Chicago — of course! He started calculating at
top speed. Before his grandparents had moved to Sainte-Mary
to be near Allan, Grandpa had owned a grocery store in
Chicago. He was nearly eighty now, so he would have been too
young to be working in 1932. On the other hand, Grandpa's
father had bought the store in 1919, right after World War I, if
Sam remembered correctly. *In other words, there must have been
Faulkners in Chicago in 1932!*

"The Faulkner grocery store, honey child? There must be
at least two thousand grocery stores in the city. I don't know
them all!"

"Do you know how we could get the address?"

"Are you sure they'll help you? Because you can stay here
for a couple of days, you know. I'm used to it. And you look so
peaked! Matthew isn't here very often, and —"

"I'd rather see them right away," Lily said.

The old lady hesitated. "Promise me you'll drink your tea
and eat your cookie, at least? And put on something besides
that nightgown thing."

"With pleasure, Mama Lucy."

"Well, that's settled! I have a nephew not far from here who just got himself a telephone. He's sure to have a directory. Any business worth its salt will be in the phone book, isn't that right?"

For the first time since their arrival in Chicago, a little color crept into Lily's face.

CHAPTER THIRTEEN

Gangsters, Firecrackers, and Kidney Beans

Locating the Faulkner grocery store turned out to be no walk in the park: Mama Lucy's nephew had a phone, all right, but no phone book to go with it. Still, he agreed to send one of his daughters to the post office, and she came back with the address. The Faulkner store was located on Irving Park Road, right where it crossed Cicero Avenue.

While they waited for the girl, Mama Lucy had plenty of time to tell Sam and Lily the history of the neighborhood, from the arrival in Chicago of the thousands of black families fleeing racism in the South, to the crowding in the shanty-towns and the start of the worst economic crisis anyone had ever seen. As she talked, she rummaged in one of her baskets to put together decent outfits for them. Lily got a lace-trimmed blue dress that was a little short but practically new. For Sam she found a worn pair of knickerbocker pants, a yellow shirt, and an orange vest. The clash of colors was so jarring that Sam was tempted to put on sunglasses.

Mama Lucy also gave them sandals, and as a bonus, a little stuffed zebra that once belonged to one of her foster children.

"This way you'll think of me from time to time," she said, handing it to Lily. "His name is Zeb, and he's eased many a heartbreak."

Lily thanked her and hugged it tight. She wasn't looking very well, and seemed to have somehow shrunk in the course of the afternoon. Mama Lucy's molasses cookies had brought a little pink to her cheeks, but she soon lapsed into an exhausted silence. As they were leaving, the old lady again suggested that they at least spend the night, but Lily jumped up, claiming she felt much better.

Sam didn't know quite what to think. He was concerned for his cousin, as she certainly didn't seem in great shape. On the other hand, he was in a hurry to get to the Faulkner grocery store. Given their situation, who would be more likely to help them than family? If worse came to worst and their great-grandparents turned them away, they could always come back to Mama Lucy's.

With the address and a rough map in hand, Sam and Lily set out early in the evening. They detoured by the construction site, where they saw the crew still working on the ruins of the house, with no chance for them to get inside. Then they headed south along the main avenues.

As they left the vacant lots and poorer neighborhoods behind, Chicago began to look like a real city, with signs, lights, tall buildings, and constant streams of pedestrians. Antique cars *put-putted* down the streets, looking comical with their square shapes and rear-mounted spare tires, making loud *ahooga!*s when they honked at intersections.

"Now those are real cars!" exclaimed Sam. "A lot cooler than Rudolf's four-by-four, don't you think?"

"Don't talk to me about Rudolf," said Lily breath-lessly. "I can't even imagine what state my mom's in! She probably gulped her whole bottle of tranquilizers down at once. But I wish she were with us," she added, sounding homesick.

It was at this point that they got lost. Disoriented by the strange noises and the mass of identical buildings, they took the wrong street, then walked around in circles until a young woman standing in a soup-kitchen line gave them directions. She nodded toward Cicero Avenue while her children tugged at her sleeves, crying for bread. Mama Lucy hadn't been lying when she described the desperate shape the country was in.

Once they were back on the right track, Sam and Lily headed straight for Irving Park. As the shadows length-ened, they admired the thousands of little lights that began to dot the city, like so many stars fallen onto Chicago's sky-scrapers. Sam craned his neck this way and that, trying to recognize a church or a monument, but he'd only been five or six years old on his single visit to the former Faulkner grocery store — a pilgrimage to the United States that Grandpa had organized — and he remembered almost nothing.

"There!" whispered Lily, pointing to a triangular block of houses at the junction of three streets. "It looks just like the photo in the album."

Indeed, a store with plate-glass windows stood at the cor-ner, with a sign written in handsome lettering:

Fine Groceries
James A. Faulkner

"James Adam Faulkner," said Sam, his voice quavering. "Grandpa's father!"

"What do we do now, Sam? We can't just show up and say, 'Hi, we're your great-grandchildren. Do you happen to know how to send us back to our own time?'"

Sam considered it. This part of Irving Park was pretty quiet, unlike what it would become later: "The busiest intersection in Chicago!" Grandpa claimed. There were just two streetlights, their meager light brightened occasionally by the headlights of passing cars. The tobacconist across the street had already closed, and the grocery store's steel shutter was lowered halfway. From the sound of voices, however, there were still people inside, and a few lights shone within.

"We better go in before the store closes," suggested Lily.

"Do you remember that stuff about the basement window?" asked Sam.

"The basement window?"

"Yeah, when Grandpa told us about being a kid. When he came home too late, he would slip in through the basement instead of the front door to avoid his father."

"So what?"

"He said the bars over the window were loose, so . . ."

"Are you saying we should break into our great-grandfather's store?"

"If we just walk in like this, what are we going to tell him? We can get into the basement through the window. That'll give us someplace to hang out while we figure out what to do next. Besides, if we spy on them for a little while, it might give us some ideas."

Secretly Sam was hoping they would find a stone statue in the basement. He knew it was unlikely, and that his father had been the first Faulkner time traveler, but there was no reason why a taste for adventure shouldn't pass from one generation to the next!

Lily didn't have the energy to argue with him, so the basement window it was. They strolled up the block until they spotted the window, which was at ground level. Somebody crossed the street just as Sam was leaning over to touch the bars, and they quickly huddled against the wall, but the passerby disappeared onto a nearby porch. There were also two cars and a truck parked down the street, but they were empty. Sam crouched down again and shook the bars. They gave a little bit, but only a little. He stood up and pulled, and to his surprise, the whole frame lifted free of the wall, inch by inch. Sam removed it from the window opening and carefully set it on the ground. He climbed in first, then helped his cousin join him before pulling the window back into place. The basement room smelled pleasantly of coffee and spices, but it was so dark that they couldn't see a thing.

"Don't budge, Lily," he whispered.

He cautiously made his way among the barrels and the sacks. Suddenly his foot caught on a crate full of bottles, causing a deafening crash. Sam froze. The noise was loud enough to be heard all over Chicago, not to say New York!

A few seconds passed. They heard footsteps on the sidewalk. Someone was walking toward the basement window! The steps slowed when they reached the window, and in the faint light Sam could make out a pair of polished shoes with white tips. Then the shoes moved away.

"Sammy, are you sure that —"

"*Shhh!*"

Sam groped his way toward the thin ray of light showing under the door, put his hand on the handle, and twisted it, holding his breath. The well-oiled knob turned easily, and he cracked the door open. A little light now reached the back of the basement, and they could hear voices upstairs.

". . . the cops? Why not the army, while you're at it? Don't you know what's what, Faulkner? We're the ones who pay off the cops!"

The tone was sarcastic, almost sadistic. Sam couldn't see beyond the bottom few steps, but he knew right away that they'd come at a bad time.

"Lookit what happened ta Wilson," said another voice, sounding hoarse from years of cigarettes and alcohol. "You know Wilson, the newspaper seller on Milwaukee Avenue, doncha? Whaddya think happens ta him? A fire! Everything goes up in smoke — *pfft!* You shoulda seen him, luggin' buckets a' water, yelpin' about freedom of the press! But freedom's got a price, don't it, Faulkner?"

"You won't get a red cent out of me," said a third voice feverishly.

Sam had no trouble identifying that one. It had Grandpa's tone and a warmth that reminded him of his own father, but a different timbre. Wasn't this the period when Al Capone and his gang terrorized the city — shaking down business owners, among other things? Sam had seen enough movies to know what was going on: James Faulkner was in trouble with the Chicago mob.

"Faulkner, Faulkner — be reasonable. It's just insurance, ya see. It's important ta have insurance! The world's a dangerous place, ya know? Anythin' can happen!"

Crash! Something, maybe a glass jar, shattered on the floor upstairs.

"Sorry, Faulkner. I'm so clumsy!"

This was followed immediately by the sound of a slap.

"Oops! Beg your pardon, Faulkner. I didn't mean ta do that!"

Lily crept up behind Sam. "We can't let them get away with this," she whispered urgently. "We have to call the police."

"The police?" Sam whispered back. "I'm not sure they would help us." He looked around for some sort of weapon, an axe handle or a stick. It would be pathetic, but just in case . . .

"What's twenty dollars a month, Faulkner?" the sadistic voice continued. "To have a store with real good insurance? Especially when you got a nice little family to take care of? You gotta think about their future!"

"You have no right to — *ow!*" Someone had thrown a punch.

Sam walked over to the shelves. One of the crates was labeled "Fireworks."

"Today is June thirtieth," he said quietly. "Independence Day in the United States is July fourth." He carefully lifted the lid, revealing supplies for the celebration: rockets of various sizes and bags of firecrackers. "We need some matches! Quick!"

As they rummaged around, an uneven battle broke out upstairs.

"Here!" said Lily.

She was shaking a paper bag whose contents made the unmistakable sound of matches rattling in their boxes.

"Go stand in a corner," urged Sam. "I'm going to try and make those slimeballs leave."

He grabbed two strips of firecrackers and went back out the basement window. The street wasn't empty — in fact, several cars were driving along it — but Sam didn't care; they might even help his plan. He walked around to the store, lit the first fuse, then yelled as loud as he could: "This is the police! Surrender! You're surrounded!"

It sounded more like a cartoon caption than a police raid, but so what? Sam ran back as the firecrackers began to pop: *Bang-bang-bang-bang!*

"Come out with your hands up!" he shouted.

Then he lit the second strip of firecrackers and heaved it as far as he could down the street. The cars driving up the street slammed on their brakes and honked their horns: *Ahooga! Bang! Bang! Ahooga! Bang!* It was a lively Fourth of July concert — a few days early!

Sam dove back into the basement and hid.

"Son of a gun!" shouted the man with the raspy voice. "What gives?"

"Out the back way!" ordered the sadist. "We ain't done with you yet, Faulkner!"

Sam and Lily heard running in the hallway overhead, going toward the back of the store.

"C'mon, step on it!"

A bolt slammed, and the footsteps were now pounding down the sidewalk outside. Sam counted to five, then headed up the stairs. The gangsters had taken off, and the glass door leading to a courtyard behind the buildings was ajar. He closed and latched it. Shouts and swearing came from the street, and Sam and Lily went to look out the window. Somebody fired a shot — a real one this time — and a car roared away.

Sam walked back into the store with Lily on his heels. The room had been turned upside down, with drawers opened, windows smashed, and damp flour and shards of glass everywhere. But there was no sign of James Faulkner. What had they done with him?

"Aaah . . ."

The moan came from behind the counter, and they hurried over to it. Kneeling on the floor, his nose bloodied, was their great-grandfather, rubbing the back of his neck as he gradually gathered his wits.

"Who . . . who are you?" he asked, trying to stand.

"We were passing by the store," Sam improvised. "There seemed to be some fighting inside, and we thought they might be robbers. We threw some firecrackers to scare them."

"Firecrackers?" James Faulkner grimaced as he felt his badly swollen upper lip. "You scared them with firecrackers? That's a hoot! How did you get in?"

"By the front door," said Lily. "In fact, it might be a good idea to lower the shutters. It would be safer."

"No. My . . . my wife is at the movies. She'll be back soon." Then, as he surveyed the extent of the damage: "Those dirty rats! They smashed everything! I'm going to call the mayor! And the newspapers too! People have to know what's going on in this city! And the police! They can't act as if I don't exist, can they? Owww . . ."

He staggered and had to be content with sitting down on a stool near the cash register. To Sam and Lily, encountering James Faulkner was almost beyond belief. Sam had seen a black-and-white photograph of him a couple of times, when he'd tried to please Grandma by pretending to be interested in the family photo albums. The picture showed the grocer with his apron, standing a little stiffly in front of his store. He was of medium height, with a handlebar mustache — a total stranger. There were also a couple of stories told about him, which Sam only half remembered. One was about a dog that escaped from the trenches in World War I; the other had something to do with his not being at his best at his wedding, with a bottle in one hand and whipped cream smeared on his jacket. And here was James Faulkner himself in person!

"We can help you straighten up if you like," Sam offered.

"Thanks. If Ketty sees this mess, she'll go out of her mind with worry. There are mops in the closet in the back. I'll give you a few coins for your trouble!"

Sam and Lily exchanged a glance, but made no comment. Instead, they got busy with mop and broom — Sam seemed destined to do housework in every era! — while James Faulkner dabbed water on his face and swathed himself in bandages.

Lily was gasping from her exertions when someone rapped on the metal shutter a quarter of an hour later.

"Daddy, it's us! We're back from the movies!"

James Faulkner worked the shutter mechanism to pull it up, and a little boy jumped into his arms, laughing.

"It was so funny, Daddy! You should've come! Charlie beat them all up!"

Sam felt his heart tighten: This was Grandpa — *their* grandpa! — when he was still a little boy!

"What happened to your nose, Daddy?"

The emotion was too much for Lily. She took a step backward, sighed like a leaky balloon, and collapsed in a dead faint on a sack of kidney beans.

CHAPTER FOURTEEN

105 Degrees

The fever lasted two days and nights. Lily's cheeks and forehead were sweaty, her teeth chattered, and she could hardly move. Responding to the family's urgent call, a doctor examined her carefully, muttered a few perplexed *"Hmms,"* and eventually admitted that he was stumped. There seemed to be nothing wrong with Lily's throat, lungs, or lymph nodes, and no inflammation was visible. It was a medical mystery — except that Lily was burning up!

"It's out of my hands," said the doctor with a fatalistic shrug.

By the middle of the second night, it didn't look as if Lily was going to live. Despite damp towels and cold compresses, her temperature rose to 105 degrees, which seemed more than her small body could stand. Sam wondered whether the inexplicable fever was a result of time-traveling. Maybe Lily couldn't endure it, being away from her original time for too long. Was her body rebelling against the wrenching leaps through the ages? If that was the case, then no cure existed. And if Lily died . . .

Sam preferred not to think about that. He had dragged her into this whole business, and she had supported him from the very beginning, far beyond anything he could have hoped for. She'd scoured the library for information about Dracula, translated the excerpt from the Bruges alchemist's book of spells, and been catapulted through time while trying to warn Sam about the police. And then there was the masterful way she had saved him from Death-eye and his clan. What would Sam have accomplished without her? If he were to lose Lily now, after losing his father and mother too . . .

Best not to think about it.

Luckily, their Faulkner great-grandparents turned out to be wonderful, especially Ketty. When she learned of the attack on her husband and the role Sam and Lily had played in his rescue, she immediately offered to take them in. She was the one who insisted on calling the doctor; then she installed Lily and Sam in the guest room, and didn't let two hours pass without bringing the patient a glass of orange juice, a treat, a picture book, or at least some words of comfort. Ketty looked severe and subdued in the album photos, but in person she was as nurturing as a mother hen, loving and attentive. Besides, she cooked hamburger steak with fried onions better than anyone!

James was harder to fathom. After the episode with the mob, he bought a black Browning pistol and two boxes of bullets and stored them under the cash register. From time to time, when the grocery store was empty, he would pull the gun out and aim at a bottle of oil or a jar of stewed fruit. Despite his wife's urging, he decided not to go to the mayor's office or the police, saying this would only attract reprisals.

Sam suspected he was just waiting for the gangsters to come back so he could take justice into his own hands.

He also had some peculiar habits. When Ketty was minding the store, James would sometimes head down to the basement without a word. Sam was intrigued — was there a connection with the stone statue? — and on the second afternoon he followed him. Surprise: His great-grandfather was sneaking out through the basement window! He was the one who had rigged the frame! When James came back half an hour later, he smelled faintly of liquor. Sam kept quiet about it, of course, but he wondered: Was this why Ketty always looked so melancholy in the family photos?

And then there was Grandpa — or as they called him, Donovan. Sam still couldn't get used to the idea. Nothing in life prepares you for playing tag with your grandfather when he's six and a half! Donovan was a sweet, helpful boy who spent most of his time playing in the courtyard with his wooden train, building level crossings and tunnels out of left-over crates, cans, and empty bottles.

"*Choo-choo!* All aboard! All aboard! Train leaving the Chicago station! Sam, you wanna be the conductor?"

Torn between incredulity and tenderness, Sam looked at his diminutive grandfather. He would have loved to take Donovan onto his lap and whisper a few scraps of his history in his ear. But he knew very well that any carelessness in the past was likely to change the future, and Grandpa's future was — Sam himself! So he kept quiet, content to watch the train as it raced between the cans.

"*Choo-choo!* Look out for the tunnel!"

Donovan was also very interested in Lily. He wasn't allowed to enter her room — she might be contagious — but he picked her flowers morning and night and made drawings for her.

"You'll give this one to Lily, won't you?" he said, holding out a sheet with a big multicolored sun. "Is she going to get better? Will we play trains together?"

The first signs of improvement appeared on the third day, when the fever began to break. Lily was able to sit propped up with pillows to eat some bread and jam and drink a glass of milk. But she was still very pale, and every sentence she spoke seemed to exhaust her meager strength.

"I'll . . . I'll pull through, Sammy. Don't look like that! You have to go see about the stone statue at the construction site."

The construction site . . . Sam had put off going there, partly because he didn't want to leave his cousin, partly for fear of what he would find. But it was indeed high time. So early that afternoon he screwed up his courage, left Lily in Ketty's competent hands, and headed up Cicero Avenue toward the black neighborhood. First he swung by Mama Lucy's to thank her for her generosity and tell her about Lily. But the old lady wasn't there — the house was closed — so he had no reason to postpone his visit to the site.

Alas, the situation was even worse than he imagined. In the space of two days, workmen had poured a flat cement slab exactly where the house once stood — probably a parking lot for the tenants of the future building. Sam spent a long time with his face pressed to the fence, praying for a miracle: that the earth would open up, say, and the stone statue would shoot out of the ground like a rocket and gently land next to him. But the only things flying around were the clouds of dust raised by the steam shovels and the orders the foremen shouted to their workers.

Figuring he had nothing to lose, Sam went to the entrance to look around, but was quickly sent packing by one of the cement workers: "Hey, you! The Yellow Kid! You got no business around here, so scram!"

He was about to head for home when he noticed a shiny black van parked a little way down the road between two earth-moving machines. The van bore a large white sign on its side: "The Collector's Paradise, Antiques, East 63rd Street & Cottage Grove Ave., Chicago." Below this was the store logo: a pair of Egyptian horns encircling a solar disk.

"Unbelievable!" he muttered.

He walked around the van. The back was closed, and he couldn't see much of anything through the driver's window. He tried the door handle, but the vehicle was locked.

"Hey, Yellow Kid!" somebody shouted behind him. "What're you up to now? Didn't I tell you to clear out?" It was the cement worker from the site.

"You mean this isn't my car?" exclaimed Sam. "Oh, *right!* That's why the key doesn't fit."

"I'll fit my fist to your nose, you see if I don't!"

Now the man was striding toward him: The two of them clearly didn't share the same sense of humor. Sam decided against a second joke and opted for a sprint instead, running to a busy street where he was able to lose his pursuer.

As he caught his breath, Sam thought about the sudden profusion of strange Us: the Sainte-Mary burglar, the

Mother-stone cave, the Pompeii pool, and now an antique shop in Chicago. Was the store a forerunner of Arkeos? Perhaps the answer was waiting for him at the intersection of 63rd Street and Cottage Grove Avenue.

After asking for directions, Sam took the trolley, paying with some of the change James Faulkner had given him. Thirty minutes and two transfers later, he got off in front of the Tivoli Theatre in a street full of businesses and restaurants, with double-parked cars and people crossing every which way. The Collector's Paradise was on the ground floor of a big hotel; the shop window was crammed with knickknacks, clocks, gold watches, and Greek and Roman statuettes identified by little tags. The company logo was painted across the window. Less stylized than Arkeos's, it had little flourishes at the ends of the horns and some discreet shading on the sun. Sam pushed open the door, which set off a rather sinister ringing of bells.

The store was a strange jumble of objects set down here and there, on the floor and on shelves, in no discernible order. An older woman with an oddly round face and sharp eyes stood peering at him from behind a counter. To Sam, she looked just like an owl.

"What can I do for you?" she asked stiffly, no doubt figuring that a boy dressed with so little care — or taste — wasn't likely to add much to her bottom line.

"I'm looking for a present for my father."

"A present for your father?" she repeated. "You're sure you're in the right place? There's a Salvation Army thrift store right next door. Isn't that what you're looking for?"

Go ahead and call my father a hobo, you old biddy.

"Actually, he collects coins," said Sam smoothly.

"Collects coins? Is that so?" she said. "Don't you think he ought to use some of them to buy you a decent shirt?"

Don't get angry, Sam reminded himself. Instead, he tried to remember some of the terms he learned on the money changers' benches in Bruges. "He especially likes Venetian ducats, florins, and Strasbourg gros."

"Strasbourg gros, eh?" said the antique seller, sounding half convinced. "Well, I suppose so . . . I'll show you what I have."

Without taking her eyes off him, she went over to a glass-fronted cabinet displaying medals and ceramics. The woman pulled out a drawer with several rows of ancient coins in more or less good shape, but unfortunately, none of them had holes. Even if Sam managed to find another stone statue, how could he and Lily get home without the coins they needed? He made a show of examining a few of the coins before putting them back on the red velvet.

"These aren't exactly the kind of coins my father collects," he declared. "But you have a very attractive logo on the window. Can you tell me what it stands for?"

"An attractive *what?*" asked the woman, rolling her owl eyes.

"The symbol under the store's name. It's a kind of head-piece that Egyptian gods wore, isn't it?"

If Sam hoped to impress her with his knowledge, he failed miserably. "If you know the answer, what's the point of asking the question?"

"I would've liked to know why you chose that symbol instead of something else," he insisted. "That's all."

"I wasn't the one who chose it," she snapped irritably. "Besides, what business is it of yours?"

The woman slammed the coin drawer shut and retreated behind her counter, brushing past a stand bearing a crystal goblet that reminded Sam of something.

"So, boy, have you made up your mind?" she continued. "Is there something here you'd like? Yes or no?"

Sam tried not to get flustered. If the antique seller hadn't chosen the logo herself, that must mean somebody else owned the business.

"Was the design chosen by the person who's at the construction site? I saw your store's van parked next to it."

The woman didn't answer right away. Instead, her eyes widened further and a nervous tic tugged at the corner of her mouth — or her beak. She looked almost frightened.

"A construction site? What construction site?" she asked uncertainly.

Sam was feeling his way now. What kind of information did he hope to get? Was the antique seller aware of the stone statue's existence? And would she be prepared to tell him about it?

"The construction site in the colored neighborhood," he said. "It's strange that somebody from your store would be interested in old houses getting torn down. I mean, there probably aren't a lot of archeological finds there."

"I don't understand a thing you're talking about!"

Sam decided to go for broke. "The guy with the van wouldn't have that symbol tattooed on his shoulder, by any chance?"

This last suggestion had a radical effect on the woman. She abruptly ducked under her counter, and for a moment Sam thought she had fainted. But she popped back up immediately, an antique musket in her hands.

"You dirty little louse!" she snapped, pointing the flared muzzle at him. "Where did you come from? And what are you up to, sneaking around the construction site?"

Sam quickly stepped to one side, putting himself behind the stand with the crystal goblet. He hoped the antique seller would think twice before blowing everything to bits.

"I was just out for a walk," he said. "I wasn't doing anything wrong."

"So who sent you, then?" she screamed. "I'm warning you, I'll shoot! You won't be the first little thief shot while trying to rob an honest business. You tell me who told you about the work site and the tattoo, or else!"

But her threats were suddenly drowned out by the tinkling music of the bells: a customer. The antique seller quickly hid her weapon under the counter, and Sam bolted for the door, nearly bowling over a distinguished-looking well-dressed man with a monocle. Ignoring the man's protests, he raced outside and sprinted up the next street.

He hadn't learned much about the strange U, but he had gotten something much more valuable: an idea for getting back to the present! Because he now remembered what the vase on the stand reminded him of: the crystal goblet belonging to the explorer Jacques Cartier, the one Garry Barenboim had willed to the Sainte-Mary Museum! Barenboim, Sainte-Mary! Sainte-Mary, Barenboim! Why hadn't he thought of that before?

CHAPTER FIFTEEN

All Aboard

The huge hall of the Chicago train station, which was hung with red, white, and blue pennants, echoed with the lively notes of a jazz band and the hurried steps of travelers.

"Are you really sure you want to leave now?" Ketty Faulkner asked.

"I feel fine," Lily reassured her. "I'm not tired at all anymore."

It was true that Lily's recovery had been as inexplicable as her illness. When Sam got back to the grocery store after his escapade at the Collector's Paradise, he found his cousin sitting on the edge of her bed, about to tackle a stack of pancakes with syrup and a big glass of apple juice. The next night passed without fever, and though Lily still looked a bit pale, she was standing very straight under the track information panels and making an admirable effort to appear healthy.

"So much the better!" exclaimed James Faulkner. "Do you have your tickets and your train schedule? The train leaves in fifteen minutes!"

Sam nodded, holding up the papers in question. "I don't know how we can ever thank you, Mr. and Mrs. Faulkner. Your putting us up, the money you lent us . . ."

"I still think you should wait a day or two," said Ketty. "If Lily's fever comes back during the trip . . ."

"Our family has been expecting us for four days," said Lily. "They must be really worried."

Which in fact wasn't far from the truth.

With perfect timing, Donovan appeared just then to change the course of the conversation.

"Mommy, look! The new Pacific 231! I've never seen such a big train! And it smokes! It smokes a *lot*!"

"Sam and Lily are leaving, darling. It's time to say good-bye to them."

"So you're going away for real?" asked the little boy.

Lily nodded and bent down to him. From her pocket she took the little stuffed zebra Mama Lucy had given her a few days earlier. "Here, Donovan, this is a present for you. His name is Zeb, and he's healed many a heartbreak." She smiled a little to hear herself repeating Mama Lucy's words. "If you ever feel sad, hug him tight and think about us, and you'll feel better." She kissed him very gently on both cheeks and stood up, on the verge of tears.

"Let's go!" said James. "It would be too bad if you missed your train."

The farewells continued on the platform as Ketty gave the children a final flurry of advice, as well as a bundle of food wrapped in a gingham cloth. After a last good-bye, they climbed into car number seven and sat down on the first available bench. Lily buried her face in her handkerchief to hide her feelings.

"All aboard!" cried the conductor as he rang his bell. "All aboard!"

With a powerful jet of steam and a deafening clanking of rods and pistons, the train got under way, gradually picked up speed, and clattered through the center of the city like a molten metal snake. Sam and Lily were quiet as the last buildings disappeared behind them and the train headed across open countryside.

"Do you think we can do it?" Lily asked at last.

Sam unfolded the sheet on which he had written the stages of their trip. "It looks okay on paper. This train will take us to Toronto, then we change to the local for Sainte-Mary. We'll be there tomorrow at the latest."

"That wasn't what I meant, Sam."

She was looking at him with her bright eyes, in which he could see both anxious concern and steely determination.

"You mean, do you think we can find the stone statue?"

She nodded, as if the question was obvious.

"I think so," he said. "We know Barenboim was using it at the start of the twentieth century, because the coins displayed at the museum and those rumors about all his strange visitors prove it. And the stone was still in the basement a hundred years later, so there's no reason to think it moved in the meantime."

"What about the coins? How are we going to manage that?"

Sam looked at the ceiling. "We still have to figure that one out. Barenboim left his collection to the city, so I'm hoping we'll be able to get hold of it."

"Doesn't it seem odd that we haven't picked up a single coin so far? You told me once that to make the stone statue work, there had to be a coin near the statue at the place you were going. That's what happened on your previous trips, right? But we haven't seen a single one!"

Sam had been wrestling with that very conundrum since his lively discussion with the lady antique seller, and had finally come up with a theory.

"I've been thinking hard about that, Lily. There weren't any coins in the cave or the Pompeii baths, or here in Chicago, but the Arkeos logo was there each time, remember? It was on the cave wall, at the bottom of the pool, and on the Collector's Paradise van."

"So what does that tell us?"

"I think the Arkeos man put those symbols there to be sure he could travel directly to certain periods. That way, instead of landing wherever the stone chooses to send him, he has a bunch of stopping places in Time — places where he left his mark. How that works, I have no idea. But I can't think of any other explanation for the way the horns and the solar disk keep showing up."

"It would certainly explain the antique store," admitted Lily. "He wouldn't have set it up if he wasn't sure he could always return to Chicago in 1932."

"I bet he supplies the old lady at the store with his finds and then invests his profits somewhere else. Maybe he even used that money to start Arkeos."

"But if the symbol always takes a time traveler to certain periods, why didn't you ever see it before?"

Sam was quiet for a minute as he mulled this over. "Here's what I think. For the system to work, the Egyptian sign has to be present at both the departure and the arrival place, sort of like a wire stretched between the times. It's like the coins, see? You need one to take off and one to land. And I think that explains the tattoo on the guy's shoulder. He had the symbol that lets him time-travel put onto his body so he could always get back to those specific times. And that would explain why the antique seller got so upset when I mentioned the tattoo. It's the key to the whole setup!"

"Like a built-in ticket to the right places," said Lily approvingly. "I understand. But what about us?" She touched his arm. "You haven't gone and gotten a tattoo, as far as I know. So why have we been finding this sign all along our route?"

"That's where it gets complicated," said Sam, leaning forward. "I've thought it over, and I have a hunch I was tricked at the museum."

"How do you mean, tricked?"

"Well, after we fought and the alarm went off, the Arkeos man rushed to the display case. I thought he wanted to steal coins and he just forgot one — the really worn one with the symbol. But afterward, when I thought about it again . . ." Sam paused to scratch his forehead, then continued: "I think he put the coin there on purpose for me to find it!"

"*What?*"

"Listen to me. First of all, I really don't remember seeing this design on any of the museum's coins that afternoon. That's weird, don't you think? I know you have to look really close to make out the horns, but I don't remember anything like it. And then that coin, the one with the Arkeos design, went with us on all of our trips, right? First in the hole in the statue, then on the sun. So is it an accident that we came across the same symbol three different times? I don't think so. This coin hasn't just gone with us through Time. I think it *guided* us to specific destinations!"

"But why would the Arkeos man want you to use it?"

"I don't know, but since he time-travels too, maybe it's a way to keep an eye on me. With that coin, at least he knows where I go."

They leaned back against the bench, weighing the implications of Sam's thinking, assuming it was correct. The train car was half full, mainly with families and couples. A little girl was running in the aisle, and a group of soldiers laughed loudly at the other end of the compartment. Small American flags hung from the ceiling, and the overall mood was cheerful. The conductor came in, followed by a very elegant young woman, then a man wearing a bowler hat.

"Just like I told you, folks. There aren't so many people in number seven."

While the conductor checked tickets, the man in the bowler went to sit near the soldiers. The young woman headed for the bench facing Sam and Lily.

"Do you mind?" she asked.

Sam helped put her suitcase on the baggage rack. She thanked him with a charming smile, then pulled a pocket mirror from her purse to fix her hair. With her straight white dress, dark glasses, and immaculate elbow-length gloves, she looked like a movie star. Sam didn't realize he was gaping until

Lily jabbed him sharply with her elbow, and he decided it might be appropriate to take a little nap.

After an hour's doze — during which Sam's thoughts drifted to a blond girl with big blue eyes — the very real smell of cold cuts pulled him from his reverie. The train was crossing hilly countryside, and Lily had spread the contents of Ketty's cloth on her lap: roast beef, sausages, salami, pickles, buns, cookies, and chocolates.

Sam made himself an extra-large sandwich with all the goodies he could pile up and began to chomp on it, avoiding the woman passenger's eye — he had his dignity, after all. It was then he noticed that the man in the bowler was up to something. From time to time, the man would turn around in his seat to steal a glance at the actress. Sam couldn't see his face, just the movement of his hat, but there was something unnerving about his spying.

"Do you want a drink?" asked Lily.

Sam took a few swallows of lemonade from the bottle, wondering what the stranger could be after. He was about to whisper to his cousin when the train roared into a tunnel. The car was plunged into darkness, and Sam felt something brush by his left side. When the light returned, the man in the bowler had disappeared. Or no, actually — he had changed seats and was now sitting right behind them, not six feet from the young woman!

Sam let his napkin fall into the aisle and leaned over to pick it up. The stranger was wearing a long, dark overcoat, its collar turned up to hide his face. He also had a strange bump at his waist — a gun? But when Sam saw the man's shoes, his stomach suddenly knotted. They were black patent leather with white tips, exactly like those he had seen outside the grocery on the night the mobsters shook down his great-grandfather. *The man in the hat wasn't after the actress: He was after them!*

"Youhavetogotothebathroom," he blurted into his cousin's ear.

"What?"

"You have to go to the bathroom right away," he repeated more clearly.

Lily looked at him with pity. "Have you lost your mind?"

Sam took their itinerary and wrote on the back: "Don't argue. The man with the hat behind us has followed us. I think he has a gun. Go to the toilet in number nine. I'll meet you."

It took Lily a moment to react. Then she stood up and casually walked to the end of the car. Sam counted to twenty to give her a head start, then, after a last smile at the actress, gathered their provisions and headed down the aisle. He opened the connecting door and found himself in the passageway that joined the two cars together. The noise was deafening, and he could see the tracks racing by under the joints in the platform — this was no time to fall through the cracks! He entered car number eight and started to run, ignoring people's stares. He did the same thing in the next car and stopped just before being smacked in the face by a black door marked "Ladies."

"Will you please tell me what you're up to?" asked Lily, popping out of the bathroom like a jack-in-the-box.

"The guy in the bowler," said Sam, gasping for breath. "He has black shoes with white tips."

"That's great! What color are his socks?"

"This isn't a joke! He was the lookout in the street the other evening when the two guys attacked Mr. Faulkner!"

"You mean he's a gangster?"

Sam grimaced. "That bump under his coat sure isn't a book of poetry!"

"But why would he follow us all this way on the train?"

"No idea! They must have been watching the grocery store. Maybe they're out for revenge."

Sam slid the vestibule door partly open to check his hunch. The stranger in the bowler had entered at the other end and was walking up the aisle, carefully studying each passenger.

"Here he comes! Let's go!"

They rushed into car nine and ran right into the conductor.

"Hey, kids, this isn't the Indy 500! Where are you running to like that?"

"My sister has diarrhea. Do you mind?"

Giving them a reproachful look, the conductor stepped aside.

"Thanks a lot," complained Lily once they were in the next passageway between cars. "That was in really great taste. Ever heard of TMI?"

"Did you want a fifteen-minute lecture? Hey, what's this?"

The next car was very different from the others. It had the quiet atmosphere of a restaurant, and about fifteen travelers were having lunch. Two waiters in white uniforms carried silver trays among the crisp white tablecloths, which hung down to the thick carpet. There were vases of fresh flowers, landscapes with lakes painted on the wall panels, and comfortable red velvet seats.

"Watch it!"

Sam caught his cousin and propelled her into the bathroom just as the conductor walked up to him.

"I don't want you hanging out in the aisles, all right?"

Wearing his most angelic expression, Sam agreed. The conductor grumbled his way forward to car eleven, and Lily was able to come out.

"Now we're stuck," muttered Sam. "The conductor in front of us, a mobster behind us! We have to . . ."

Another tunnel. The light suddenly vanished and the roar of the train made the floor shake.

"Quick!"

Sam forced his cousin to her knees and shoved her under the first empty dining car table.

"Will you quit pushing me around?"

"Quiet!" he ordered, scrunching down next to her. "He'll be here any second!"

The train emerged into the light, and Sam lifted a corner of the tablecloth to see a pair of shiny white-tipped shoes coming their way.

"Waiter!" called a hoarse, almost sandy voice.

"Would you like to have lunch, sir?" asked the waiter.

"No, I'm looking for two children, a boy and a girl. Have you seen them?"

"I'm very busy with my tables, sir."

"They were running as if the police were chasing them. You couldn't have missed them."

His tone was urgent, practically threatening. Besides the shoes, all the children could see were the bottoms of some blue canvas pants and a worn gabardine coat.

"Unfortunately, sir, when I'm working . . ."

"I understand." There was a noise like the crackle of dollar bills. "Maybe this will help."

The waiter seemed to hesitate. "Actually, now that you mention it — that's right, a boy and a girl."

Lily dug her nails into Sam's arm.

"They ran out the other end, toward the sleepers," said the waiter. "They were running fast, all right."

"Very good. If they come back, please let me know. I'm in car seven."

The polished shoes vanished from Sam's field of vision, and after a few seconds the tablecloth snapped up, uncovering them.

"Come out of there!" A brown hand reached down to them. "Stealing clothes, hiding under tables — don't you two *ever* do anything normal?"

"Matthew!" Lily cried.

The uniform, the voice . . . of course! The waiter was none other than Mama Lucy's adopted son!

Matthew shook his head. "I was watching you from the kitchen. You kids seem to attract nothing but trouble!"

"That guy belongs to a gang that attacked my grandfather's grocery store," Sam explained quietly. "They didn't get what they wanted, so they decided to come after us."

Matthew didn't seem particularly convinced. "Well, that's as may be. But if that guy is really after you, I know a place you'll be safe."

A customer at one of the far tables was getting impatient. "Waiter, please!"

"Right away, ma'am . . . Okay, I have to hurry or my boss will get mad."

He quickly led them to the other side of the car, to a compartment stacked high with sheets, tablecloths, and napkins.

"I'm in charge of linens for the sleeping and dining cars, so no one will bother you in here. There's not much room, but . . . Here, I'll give you my key. If you get too hot, just open the window."

Several hours passed before Matthew appeared again. Lily and Sam used the time to make themselves a cozy nest among the bags of linens and finish the lunch they'd started. They also came up with a couple of theories about the man with the bowler hat's real intentions, without being fully satisfied with any of them. Was he someone sent by the mob? An accomplice of the Arkeos man? The Arkeos man himself?

Finally, as night was falling, they heard a soft knock at the door.

"Open up. It's me, Matthew."

He stepped inside carrying a bundle of dirty linen.

"Your guy is a tough customer; he doesn't give up easily. He went up and down the train several times this afternoon. He even checked the toilets. Didn't put him in an especially good mood either."

"What if we told the conductor?" suggested Lily.

"Mason? He's as yellow as they come. Don't count on him for help. Are you going to Toronto?" Sam nodded. "I'll help you get off onto the tracks. No one will see a thing."

"Mama Lucy is right to be proud of you," Lily told him. "You really take after her!"

He laughed. "Don't let appearances fool you, missy. I'm helping you mainly for your politics! I don't know who tipped you off, but the Democrats chose Roosevelt and Garner for the presidential elections, just like you predicted! And I picked up a thousand dollars along the way. So if you have any other ideas along those lines . . ."

"That was just luck," said Lily. "I read an article in the newspaper."

"What paper was that? I want to subscribe!"

At his charges' looks of embarrassment, Matthew burst out laughing again. "You really are a strange pair! But I like that! Hand me that bag over there. I have to take clean sheets to the sleeping cars. When we arrive, don't budge until I come get you."

Matthew kept his word. Once the train pulled into Toronto early the next morning, he helped them off the train onto the tracks, out of sight of the other travelers. Then he said good-bye and went back to his job. He had to greet the new passengers for the trip home.

At nine o'clock in the morning, after carefully studying their surroundings, Sam and Lily finally boarded the first train headed for Sainte-Mary. There was nothing the man in the bowler could do to them now.

CHAPTER SIXTEEN

Old Acquaintances

For the first time since he started "traveling," Sam had really become aware of what the passage of Time meant. It was one thing to pay a quick visit to a time and place you knew nothing about, but quite another to meet your six-year-old grandfather or to arrive at a familiar place a century earlier. If Sam and Lily hadn't seen a big wooden sign reading "Welcome to Sainte-Mary" as they left the train station, they might have had serious doubts about where they were.

"What happened to the mayor's office?" asked Lily in amazement. "Don't they need a mayor? And what about the park?"

Sainte-Mary wasn't a city anymore; it was a large village at best. There were so few streets and buildings, it looked like a case of *Honey, I Shrunk the Town!* Only three cars — with boxy lines, rear-mounted spare tires, and the occasional *ahooga!* — were trundling along the main street, from which all modern structures had disappeared. In their place rose two-story buildings with shops on the ground floor and living quarters above. On the sidewalks — just dirt embankments, actually — vendors sold fruit and vegetables out of carts. Street lighting came from a pair of stubby wrought-iron gas lamps, a far cry from the majestic avenue of lights that would brighten twenty-first-century nights.

"Look, the DVD rental place is a men's clothing store!"

"The skating rink! It's a cow pasture!"

"And the big hotel is a public bathroom!"

The changes went on and on. Sainte-Mary looked like a rural backwater, and its crowds wore clothes that were definitely more "country" than in Chicago. But the mood in town was far from glum. People were talking loudly and calling to each other from one end of the row of stores to the other. A few citizens already seemed well lubricated with alcohol.

"At one in the afternoon, for heaven's sakes!" said Lily.

They discovered the reason for this excitement behind what would someday be the area's biggest shopping center: a muddy field where a noisy crowd was applauding a plowing contest. Two workhorses were going head to head, each dragging a clawed device that dug deep furrows in the ground. The supporters of the teams cheerfully shouted insults back and forth.

"You can see why Fontana's fields yield half as much as ours do!"

"If you want those Sainte-Mary nags to pull, you got to feed them!"

Lily asked, "So this is a kind of county fair, right?"

"Something like that," answered Sam above the hubbub. "But there's probably something else happening too. Have you ever heard of the mêlées?"

"Mêlées?"

"From what I understand, there were these big competitions between Fontana and Sainte-Mary for years. They usually ended in gigantic fights, which is why they're called mêlées. I think they usually happened at this time of year, around the first of July."

"On Canada Day?"

"Yeah. But then some people got really hurt, and the fights were banned after World War II. That's sort of how the Sainte-Mary/Fontana judo tournament got started — it's a lot more peaceful."

"So if everyone's here, this is probably the perfect time to look around the town, right?"

They briefly considered going to their school, which was quite close. But what would they find there? A potato field? A pigpen? Instead, they left the Fontana and Sainte-Mary fans' alcoholic huzzahs behind and walked over to Barenboim Street. To their surprise, they enjoyed the relaxed feeling of crossing a downtown free of the oppressive crush of traffic. Children played with jacks or hoops in the street, people stopped to greet one another, more animals could be seen — birds, especially — and the flowers smelled sweet. It might be interesting to live in a Sainte-Mary without a broadband connection and an MP3 player.

Barenboim Street felt more cheerful too. The houses were the same ones Sam and Lily knew, but their paint was a lot fresher and their gardens better tended. Also, the street had a mood of carefree simplicity Sam would never have imagined.

There was one exception to all this, however: the house they were heading for.

When they opened the gate, it creaked on its hinges. Weeds had overgrown the walkway, and the stoop was nearly hidden under piles of junk and scrap metal. A couple of windows were broken, the siding was peeling off, and a weather vane listed sadly on the roof.

"Is this a haunted house set or what?" Lily whispered.

They reached the front door, which swung slightly in the breeze. Gone were the scent of flowers and the chirping of birds, replaced here by the stench of stale beer and clogged toilets.

Sam entered the house first. The main room, where his father would set up his bookshelves seventy-five years later, was littered with wood scraps, broken bottles, and cigarette butts. Someone had apparently started a fire under a window once, and the flames had scorched the wall and blackened the ceiling.

"It looks awful," said Lily, glancing around the room, "but we'd have more problems if someone was living here, right?"

Sam nodded as they headed toward the basement. But just then a teenage boy with a cigarette dangling from his mouth stepped out of the darkened stairway leading upstairs.

"You were right, Bradley, we've got company," he said.

Four or five other teenage boys stood behind him. The speaker blew smoke in Sam and Lily's faces.

"Monk," he said. "Go see if anybody else is coming."

Sam felt a jolt of electricity shoot up his spine. How could big Monk, who had nearly flattened him at the judo tournament, be here in 1932? But it was a lanky boy with downcast eyes who got to his feet and went to check the front door.

When he returned, he announced somewhat wearily: "I don't see anyone out there, Paxton."

Paxton? Was Paxton in on this too?

"Perfect," said the first boy. "We'll be able to talk quietly. Upstairs, everyone!"

At a sign from him, the others surrounded Sam and Lily and crowded them toward the steps.

"What do you think you're doing?" Sam began. "We aren't going anyplace with you!"

Paxton stepped to within a few inches of Sam and jabbed his finger at him. He was smaller than his descendant — Alicia's Jerry Paxton — and had a long scratch across his forehead and a badly chipped tooth on the side of his mouth. Sam suspected they weren't going to be great pals.

"You're on my turf here and you do what I say. Get it?"

Lily shot him a glance begging him not to resist, and Sam allowed himself to be led upstairs. The rooms had been turned into a crash pad. There were mattresses on the floor, a pile of empty bottles, and garbage everywhere. *This is my house,* Sam raged silently, though he knew the thought was absurd. *You might treat it a little better!*

Paxton dropped into a battered armchair while his lieutenants flanked the two intruders. "So you're from Fontana, eh?"

"No, we're not," Sam answered.

"Well, you're not from Sainte-Mary, anyway."

That's exactly where we're from, you jerk — but there was no good way to explain. Aloud, he said, "We just came from Chicago."

"From Chicago?" A glint flashed in Jerry Paxton's grandfather's eyes. Or was it his great-grandfather or great-uncle?

Whatever the case, acting like a jerk was clearly genetic with these people.

"To me, Chicago is worse than Fontana," he said. "I wanna kill all those smart alecks from Chicago. Isn't that right, you guys?" The rest of the gang laughed raucously. "Besides, we need somebody to train on."

"Train for what?" Lily asked.

"Girls shut up!" Paxton yelled. "Especially when they're young enough to hide in their mothers' skirts! We're gonna win that mêlée this year if it kills us. Or we kill them." He grinned. "Shirts off, guys!"

As in a well-rehearsed ballet, the five punks slipped their suspenders from their shoulders and took off their shirts in unison.

"You too," Paxton told Sam.

"What about the girl?" asked Monk. "It'd be better if she didn't watch."

Paxton seemed to hesitate for a moment. "You're gettin' sentimental, Monk, ever since your old man died. But okay, lock her up. I'll deal with her later."

There was nothing very encouraging in this show of generosity. Skinny Monk grabbed Lily by the arm and dragged her out to the hallway. Meanwhile, his bare-chested buddies started circling Sam, fists clenched. He was going to be the punching bag for this afternoon's boxing practice!

To gain time, he slowly unbuttoned his shirt, while glancing right and left. The windows didn't have any panes, so he could jump down into the yard if he had to. But even if he didn't break something, Lily would still be stuck upstairs. As for facing these animals . . .

159

"Start by hitting him in the stomach and ribs," ordered Paxton, playing his role as coach to the hilt. "For his face, wait for my signal. Go!"

The order was hardly given before his adversaries all attacked at once. Sam felt as if the ceiling had crashed down on his head. This had nothing to do with boxing! He tried to stay upright for a moment, protecting himself as best he could, but soon found himself on the floor, buried under their number.

"That is enough!" shouted a hoarse voice. "I will not say it twice!"

The furor instantly subsided, and everyone turned to look at the door. Standing on the threshold was a small man with copper-colored skin, wearing a bowler hat and polished shoes with white tips. He looked to be about sixty and seemed very calm. Though Sam had never seen his face before, he had no trouble recognizing him. This wasn't a mobster or even the Arkeos man, as he had speculated on the train. It was the venerable Setni, high priest of the Egyptian god Amon, in whose tomb the first stone statue had been found. And here he was in Sainte-Mary, in the flesh!

Paxton sniggered. "Two for the price of one! We'll be in great shape for the mêlée!"

Without warning, he leaped from his chair and rushed at the small man, leading with his right foot. To Paxton's considerable surprise, Setni dodged him easily, then drew a very flexible stick from under his gabardine coat and whipped the air with it.

"I mean you no harm, you crazed young cur. Leave now, and nothing will happen to you."

"We'll see if I'm leaving," barked Paxton, throwing a terrific punch at him. But once again, Setni stepped aside as if he'd anticipated his attacker's move. *The déjà vu effect,* thought Sam, the same thing he'd experienced against the twenty-first-century Monk during their judo match. Paxton found himself off balance with his arm extended and caught a stinging crack on the chin from Setni's stick.

"This time you're dead!" he roared, purple with rage. But Paxton's next attack was no more successful than the others, and he smashed into a wall. He raised his hands to his nose, which was spurting blood.

"Get 'im, you guys!" he yelled.

His companions finally reacted and rushed the high priest. An incredible phenomenon then happened: For the space of a minute, it was as if Time slowed down. Monk and his friends seemed gripped by a strange lethargy, moving with extreme difficulty while Setni struck with his stick at astonishing speed. Even Sam felt seized by some invisible, paralyzing force; he had trouble moving or even blinking. Then with the snap of a released rubber band, Time abruptly began to flow again. The high priest stepped back. Most of his opponents were on the ground, rubbing their necks or hips, dumbfounded by what had just happened to them.

"He's a magician!" moaned a terrified Bradley. "Let's get out of here!"

The gang tumbled down the stairs, scooping up their leader on the way. Leaning on his stick and panting, Setni watched them go. He was drenched in sweat and looked haggard.

"Are you all right, sir?" Sam asked cautiously.

"Yes . . . I am fine. It is just . . . exhausting," he gasped. "I know I should not do it, but sometimes . . ."

He gradually caught his breath and Sam kept away from him, for fear of breaking some sort of spell. At last the high priest straightened up and looked him over from head to foot. "What about the girl?" he asked.

"She isn't far. I can get her."

Setni nodded and the two walked into the next room — Sam's future bedroom, in fact. It held yet more of the paltry treasures accumulated by the Sainte-Mary punks: a spare tire — one drawback of mounting them on top of the trunk! — some farm tools, a case of beer, scales with weights, and so on. Against the far wall stood a wobbly, battered wardrobe. It was apparently possessed by a ghost who was banging on the door, yelling, "Let me out!"

Sam turned the key in the lock and his cousin burst out, all teeth and claws.

"Easy, Lily! It's me!"

At the sight of the small bald man with the weathered face and the bowler, she froze. "You're —"

"I'm afraid there was a misunderstanding yesterday, miss. I had no intention of harming you in the train."

"You followed us from Chicago! Sam saw you in front of the grocery store that night with the gangsters!"

"I followed you from Chicago, that's right."

Sam spoke up. "Lily, this gentleman is Setni, the high priest."

A breath of disbelief hovered in the air. It was as if Sam had recited a very ancient and very secret incantation and summoned a genie or a ghost. The person standing before them was nearly three thousand years old! He came from a world where people built pyramids, worshipped the sun, launched golden boats on the Nile, and mummified their dead. He was the one person who might be at the origin of everything, the one who had traveled through Time further than anyone — and today he had come here to help them.

"Setni?" Lily repeated.

"It's an honor," said Sam, bowing deeply.

"Straighten up, young man," said the high priest kindly. "So, you know my name?"

"I met your son Ahmosis in Thebes."

"Ahmosis! Thebes!" the old man exclaimed. "So I was right. You have indeed been using the Thoth stone. And that is why you emerged from the demolished house."

Lily was surprised all over again. "You mean you were at the construction site too?"

"Of course! Otherwise how could I have found my way to your store? I came to the great city of Chicago to find out why that stone was going to be destroyed. For several months, something unusual has been disturbing the paths of Time, and it is my duty to discover what it is. And then I suddenly see you emerge from the ruins, with the workers all wondering where you could have popped up from."

Something unusual, thought Sam. *What if that unusual thing was me?*

"I guessed that you had pierced Thoth's secrets, and I decided to learn more about you," Setni continued. "To see if you were the cause of these perturbations, for example. You are the first children I have encountered on the paths of Time!"

"So we led you to the grocery store that evening? You didn't have any connection with the gangsters inside?"

"Of course not! I even had to, er, encourage them to leave."

"You chased them away?" exclaimed Sam and Lily together.

"No, *you* chased them away; I merely helped convince them to depart. They fired a shot in the air to frighten me, but I have some experience with combat, as these young louts discovered. In any case, that additional agitation piqued my curiosity. So I watched you for a few days and decided yesterday to approach you in the train car. I did not expect you would give me the slip!"

"How did you find us after that?"

"There are very few Thoth stones in this era and on this continent. Besides, I have often come to Sainte-Mary."

"Barenboim?" wondered Sam.

"You know Garry Barenboim!" the old man cried with delight. "You really are very surprising!"

"We've only heard about him," Lily explained, "but we know that this house belongs to him."

"And so does the stone statue," said Setni.

Sam pointed downstairs. "Speaking of the stone, I'd like to make sure it's still there."

They silently walked down to the basement. It was very dark, and they had to kick out the boards nailed across the little window to get some light and air. What they saw was appalling. It was likely that nobody had cleaned the basement since Barenboim's death some fifteen years earlier. It had a thick layer of dust, a tangle of spiderwebs, mold on the walls, at least two dead rats, and a mound of decaying garbage, some of it related to the lack of sanitary facilities they had already observed upstairs.

"This is disgusting!" said Lily, gagging.

"It is not much compared to the world's misery," answered Setni enigmatically.

They started to clear the back of the basement, where a jumble of rusty machinery prevented them from reaching its darkest corners.

"Well, is it here or isn't it?" asked Lily impatiently.

Sam frantically tossed loom parts and empty thread bobbins out of the way, his energy fueled by anxiety. Finally he shoved a pile of metal spindles aside and uncovered the stone.

"It's beautiful," Sam murmured. He stroked the statue, seeking the familiar vibration. But he felt only a distant trembling, imperceptible to the uninitiated. Something was missing. He looked up at Setni. "The problem is, we don't have a coin anymore."

The high priest's expression remained unreadable. Then he said, "Am I to understand that you have been traveling the paths of Time at random, with a single disk of Re?"

"A disk of Re?" asked Sam, feeling ill at ease. "Well, we started with three of them, but we had really bad luck and had to leave very quickly each time. Either we were in danger, or the stone was threatened. Anyway, we left our three . . . our three disks of Re behind."

The old man looked at him sternly. "Traveling that way is very imprudent, my young friends. There are many things you seem not to know, and . . ." He rubbed his bald head. "Before going any further, I think we had better talk."

CHAPTER SEVENTEEN

Revelations

They gathered in the room with the mattresses, after clearing away the empty bottles and creating a more or less clean space around the armchair. Setni took off his long gabardine and made himself comfortable, sitting cross-legged in the chair. Under the coat he wore a linen tunic and a woven belt with a long leather pouch. He occasionally glanced out the window to make sure no one was coming up the walk, though he remarked once that Paxton's gang wouldn't be back anytime soon. "They are like all cowards," he said. "Strong against the weak and weak against the strong."

For a full hour, Sam and Lily told Setni how they had discovered the stone and described the adventures they'd had up until landing in Chicago. The high priest didn't interrupt, merely nodding when the two described this or that obstacle they'd had to overcome. When their account was finished, Setni gazed into the distance, apparently lost in thought. Then he turned to Lily.

"Come here, my girl." The old man carefully examined the

166

whites of her eyes. "How many days did you say the fever lasted?"

"Three days."

"You caught Time sickness, no doubt about it. When it happened to me, I spent a week flat on my back, unable to move. Some people die of it, others never catch it. But you are now cured. You just need some rest."

He then questioned Sam about what exactly had happened when the bear attacked the stone in the cave and during the Pompeii earthquake. He also wanted to know more about the Arkeos man and the symbol, though he listened to the answers without any reaction. Finally he folded his hands under his chin and smiled gravely. "Do you know the story of Imhotep and King Djoser, children?"

Sam and Lily shook their heads.

"It happened a long, long time ago, more than eighty generations before my birth. Djoser was a wise pharaoh who had conquered many lands. He was the richest and most powerful of the world's rulers. A word from him was enough to send armies without number to attack an enemy or teams of workers to build the most magnificent palaces. Yet Djoser was unhappy. He had a daughter, Neferur, whom he loved more than anything and who suffered from an incurable illness. Each day when she awoke, her bedding was soaked through, and she was weaker and thinner than the night before, unable to speak or feed herself. Imhotep, who was the king's physician as well as his architect, tried all of the potions known in the Upper and Lower Nile. He sent men to countries near and far in the hope that someone somewhere had heard of a similar illness and knew how to treat it. But in vain.

"One evening, when Neferur was near death, Imhotep asked Djoser's permission to speak in his name to the god Thoth, who is both the most skilled of the healing gods and the juggler of hours and seasons. After the king's physician spent a night in prayer, Thoth finally agreed to help him, on the condition that Imhotep build a monument in his honor, the likes of which had never been seen in Egypt before. Imhotep swore that he would.

"'The pharaoh's daughter has but one more day to live,' the ibis-headed god told Imhotep, 'and there is no remedy in this country that can cure her. If you want to save her, you will have to travel the paths of Time in search of an appropriate medicine.'

"Imhotep agreed, and Thoth designed a stone carved with a sun that would allow him to travel to seven different eras with the help of seven disks of Re, the sun god.

"'You will have but a single day to spend visiting each of these worlds,' said Thoth, 'and each of those days will be as the seventh part of a day here. Once that day is over, if you have not returned or if you have failed, the princess will die and you will die with her. I will follow your progress on this scroll.'

"He showed Imhotep a papyrus, the scroll of Thoth, that displayed a series of hieroglyphs, always the same ones. Finally the god taught Imhotep how to carve stone statues so he could pursue his quest wherever he was. And thus, before sunrise, Imhotep set out on the paths of Time."

Setni paused, opened his leather pouch, and pulled out a sheaf of fine, rolled-up papyri. "I think the scroll of Thoth looked something like this."

The sheets were dark yellow, faded and aged, with black handwritten signs repeated in groups of thirty or forty.

"We have something like that back home," Sam said. "A Book of Time with a red cover and identical pages."

"Do you know where that book is right now?"

"In Lily's bedroom, I guess," he said. She nodded.

Setni made no comment, but didn't seem pleased by the answer.

"What about the rest?" asked Lily.

"I beg your pardon?"

"Imhotep! Where did he go in Time?"

"Oh, the rest of that story! I do not know it."

"What do you mean?" insisted Lily. "You promised us the story of Djoser, and you're stopping halfway through!"

The old man's eyes had a sly gleam. "I did not say that. The fact is, I cannot tell you the story of Imhotep's seven voyages because his account of them disappeared during the invasion by the Hyksos, barbarians from the East. We think his journal was taken out of Egypt, along with many other things. Only a small chest containing a dozen tablets was spared and hidden in the Temple of Amon."

"Where you found them," suggested Sam.

"Yes, a year after I became the high priest. The tablets were especially interesting because they explained exactly where to find the Thoth stone and how to use it."

But Lily wasn't letting Setni off the hook. "What about Neferur?"

"Neferur? Imhotep was able to bring her the medicine she needed — antibiotics from your era, I believe. And as promised, Djoser had him erect a monument unlike any seen before:

a stone pyramid, the first pyramid in Egypt! Djoser is entombed there, but it was originally dedicated to the god Thoth — something people have forgotten today. As for Neferur, she lived a long and happy life without knowing anything of her physician's exploits."

"Imhotep made seven voyages," Sam said after a few moments. "How many have you made?"

"Many, many more. How old do you think I am?"

"Sixty or sixty-five," Lily guessed.

"I am forty-seven. What you see in my face are the marks of the distress and suffering of the thousands of lives I have encountered. The world is cruel, whatever century one considers it from."

"Then why have you continued to travel?"

"Because I have no choice. As the guardian of the Thoth stones, I must watch over them and make sure no one uses them for evil purposes. I have even drawn up a map with the location of each one according to its period. It is coming along nicely. Here, take a look."

From his bag he took another scroll, which he unrolled with a hint of pride. The outlines of oceans and continents were approximately marked — probably the way Setni imagined them — and there were dozens of black and red notations. One could make out mountains in dark green; the courses of great rivers in blue, with the Nile being the most recognizable; and dots with names that might be cities or notations on the time period involved. Finally, there were a few tiny pinholes. The overall layout was beautiful but quite hard to read. According to Setni's representation, the Earth was a multicolored archipelago with vague borders.

Parts of it had apparently been explored, but most remained undiscovered.

"How many stone statues are on your map?"

"I have counted about fifty."

"About fifty!" cried Lily. "But the legend speaks of Imhotep's seven voyages. Seven voyages, seven stones, right?"

"That is also what I thought at first. But do not forget that the god Thoth, in his great wisdom, taught the architect-physician how to carve his own stones in order to help him in his research. So seven is the number of original stones. Imhotep's knowledge must have later passed on to other travelers, who in turn have seeded the wide world with stones. I know from experience that someone who travels the paths of Time feels the urge to carve the sun of Re at least once. If he chooses the place with care, and especially if his intentions are pure, the spell can work and the stone comes alive. But he who scorns Thoth's magic and carves a stone solely to become richer or more powerful never gets more than a useless piece of rock."

"Is there anything on your map that relates to Bran Castle?" asked Sam.

To answer, Setni didn't even need to consult his scroll. "I do not claim that the map is complete, unfortunately, or that it ever will be. But if you really want to find your father, there are some things you must learn, in particular about the disks of Re. The way you are using them now is too uncertain. With just one disk, your destination is in the hands of fate. You could wander the paths of Time for centuries without ever reaching Bran Castle!"

"That's exactly why I need those seven coins!" answered Sam forcefully.

"But the seven coins have a major drawback. They will indeed transport you to the desired period, but they remain behind in the one you left. So while you reach the place you want, you deprive yourself of any way to return!"

"But I managed to get back," Sam pointed out. "Several times."

"Only thanks to your cousin, my boy. Despite your ignorance of the workings of Time, you have had incredible luck. Very few humans can bring time travelers back to their point of departure. It is a power possessed by only a few women and is said to be transmitted from mother to daughter. As for developing the skill, one must be a very experienced magician. This girl was born with it."

Sam suddenly found himself looking at his cousin in a new light. It wasn't enough for just anyone in the present to be thinking about you. That someone had to have a gift — a special priceless gift — and Lily had it! She *was* a truly exceptional girl.

But Lily behaved exactly as if they were talking about someone else, keeping her eyes on Setni as she pursued her line of thought. "If you started drawing a map of the stones, that must mean there's a way to travel with certainty, right?"

Setni again reached into his leather sack and took out a kind of wooden button. He unscrewed it, and it came apart in two halves.

"This capsule was given to me by the widow of a Chinese emperor, who was about to die herself. She told me that by slipping a disk into it, the stone would take me where I wanted to go. But a capsule like this can only be used once, and I never dared try it."

"So you have a more reliable way to travel?" Lily pressed him.

The high priest stood and went to the window to look at the street.

"As I said, the legend of Djoser does not tell the whole story. To allow Imhotep to make his voyage, Thoth gave him a third gift in addition to the stone statue and the disks of Re: a jewel that the god had forged with his own hands. It was a finely worked bracelet that he called 'the golden circle.' Almost no written descriptions of it have survived. Imhotep could slip six of the seven coins onto the bracelet before fitting them into the six rays of the sun. That way, when he applied the seventh coin to the sun, he not only reached his desired destination, but all the coins made the voyage with him — even the coin in the sun. Thanks to the golden circle, Imhotep could move as he pleased among the seven times made available to him by the seven coins. It was his key to the paths of Time!"

"And that's why the coins have holes in them!" said Lily excitedly. "So they could be threaded on the golden circle!"

Driven by a sudden impulse, Sam stood and approached the high priest. "Where is it?"

Setni patted him on the shoulder. "The golden circle? To my knowledge, a copy of the original was created somewhere in the Orient, probably on the basis of Imhotep's lost account. As to who has it today . . ."

"What about the original?" asked Sam in an unusually sharp tone of voice.

"It is in my possession," answered Setni calmly. "But I will not give it to you, as you can well understand; nor will I show it to you, because it might turn your head. Its influence is unpredictable, let us say. Some have gone mad at the idea of possessing it."

Sam felt a wave of irrepressible anger rising in him. He must have this golden circle! He needed it to save his father — right away! And if this old man refused to give it to him . . .

Almost in spite of himself, he took a step closer to Setni, but the high priest stopped him with a gesture.

"I can sense your anger, my boy, but think of the treatment I gave Paxton and his gang earlier. You are not yet a match for me."

Setni's firm voice and serene expression made Sam's aggressiveness evaporate immediately. "I'm sorry," he said, feeling abashed. "I don't know what came over me. I couldn't help myself."

"The fascination exercised by the golden circle can corrupt the best-intentioned minds, my boy. Consider your anger a warning, and try to remember it in the future."

"But what's the point of explaining these things to us if it won't help us bring Sam's dad back?" asked Lily.

"In the kind of quest that you are on, my young friends, the truth is far preferable to a lie. It will allow you to make right and necessary choices when the time comes. That time will surely come, and much sooner than you may wish. Too many things are happening around you and the stone. The bear that attacked it in the cave, the earthquake that submerged and split it, those machines that buried it on the work site — do you to think that was all coincidence? A simple twist of fate? Normally, people barely notice Thoth stones, and as for animals . . ."

Setni again unrolled the map and pointed out some of the pinpricks on the papyrus to them. "For my part, a number of signs have warned me that danger was threatening the paths of Time. Look: These points correspond to places where stones have disappeared these last months. Here is the city of Vesuvius, and here is the bear clan's cave."

He pointed to two fairly widely spaced little holes on a colorful and vaguely star-shaped patch that might be Europe. "As I said, it was when visiting another of those places, in Chicago, that I made your acquaintance." He pointed to a landmass shaped like an elongated figure eight that must have been North and South America. "Having heard your story, here is what I think: I am almost sure that the Oracle of Delphi is right, and someone is trying to close the doors of Time. Someone has decided to destroy the stones to prevent you from going home."

A deathly silence followed. Sam and Lily sat petrified, as if an invisible darkness had suddenly shrouded the room.

"Des-destroy the stones?" Sam finally stammered. "You mean it's intentional? But how can someone act at a distance to keep us from coming home?"

"You have not taken proper care of your Book of Time, that is all. The book not only serves as a log of the travelers' voyages, it is directly linked to the stones. If you are traveling through Time — to 1932, for example — and some person who wishes you ill rips a page from your book, the stone through which you arrived will be destroyed. Unless you can find another stone, you would be condemned to live out your lives far from your own time."

"But the Book of Time is hidden in my bedroom," protested Lily.

"You can be sure it is no longer there, miss."

"But why come after us?" Sam asked. "We haven't done anything!"

The priest shrugged. "You may have unwittingly stirred up things beyond your understanding. Take this Arkeos man. The solar horns stand for Re's daughter Hathor, the two-faced goddess who can punish people severely or shower them with gifts. Depending on which path one takes, great good or great suffering can result. The man's ability to use this sign shows a high level of knowledge, and if he has profaned your Book of Time, as I suspect he has, it is not hard to know which path he has chosen."

"Does that mean Sam was right about the tattoo? That the Arkeos sign lets you travel to specific places?"

"Only to some extent," cautioned the high priest. "The sign of Hathor will take you to a place where you have already drawn it, but it does not let you choose a specific place among all those that exist. In other words, you may need ten attempts to reach one particular place. And the more signs there are, the greater the uncertainty."

Sam said, "What really scares me is that if the Arkeos man stole our book, that means he broke into our house. And that means Grandma and Grandpa are in danger. We have to go home as fast as we can!"

"I will not abandon you," Setni promised. "Even if your book is damaged, I have certain resources that I can draw on. You can start by taking the Chinese capsule. It will be more useful to you than to me." He handed the curious wooden button to Sam. "I will explain the rest downstairs," he added.

He headed for the stairs, with Lily at his heels.

"There's still one thing that bothers me," she said. "Can the Thoth stone send us to a period where we already are? What I mean is, is there any chance I'll run into myself at age seven or thirty-five?"

"That is very unlikely, my girl. A body is an assemblage of flesh, bone, and fluids, but a soul is completely unique. Two identical souls cannot be in the same place at the same time. If that were to happen, the soul would inevitably consume itself, unless the traveler were in a hypnotic trance or a magic sleep, perhaps. But otherwise . . ."

"That's good!" said Lily. "I'd hate to see myself twenty years older!"

They stepped into the basement, and Setni again rummaged in his sack.

"This should do the trick. As I told you earlier, an experienced magician can use his own book to send a traveler back to his or her starting place. I doubt that two travelers will be much more difficult than one." He handed Sam a coin.

Sam took the disk of Re in his fingers. It was an ordinary coin, with plant designs twining around the hole in the center, but it gave off a characteristic warmth.

"You are saving our lives, high priest."

"That is also my role, as a servant of Amon. And speaking of which . . ." He stared at Sam, and for just a moment, Sam had the feeling that an invisible hand was touching his brain. It was frankly unpleasant.

"I am getting older," the high priest said gently as he dropped his gaze. "Time is irreversibly wearing me down. I can feel it. And I am not immortal, as you know from visiting my tomb in Thebes."

Sam would have liked to reassure Setni about his age, to tell him that he still had many years to live, but the priest raised two fingers to prevent him.

"Shhh, my boy! I do not desire to know anything about my death, either what precedes or what follows it. That is one of the conditions of fulfilling my task honestly. But whatever happens, the Thoth stones will need a new guardian someday. Someone with enough strength to resist the temptations the traveler faces, enough heart to distinguish good from evil, and enough judgment to keep the course of Time from being changed. This last point is especially crucial. A series of infinite catastrophes could follow if someone decided to change the unfolding of the world — someone like your Arkeos man, for example, who uses the sign of Hathor for his own profit. That is why there must always be someone to guard the stones. And I am convinced that you, Samuel Faulkner, would be worthy of fulfilling that function."

"Me?" Sam blinked. "But I just want to save my father and go home! That's it!"

"Of course, of course," said Setni. "It is too soon, much too soon! But think about it, and when the time comes . . . Well, make what you feel is the right decision."

The high priest took a step toward them. "It is now time for you to leave, my children. You are still far from the end of your road, and many other paths await you!"

He held them briefly in his arms, then led them to the stone. As Sam knelt to put the coin in the center of the sun, he couldn't help asking one last question, the one that had been on the tip of his tongue. "Will we see each other again someday?"

Setni's expression was unfathomable. "Probably not in the way you imagine, young man."

CHAPTER EIGHTEEN

A Matter of Trust

Sam slumped onto his side and remained prostrate for a moment, unable to move. He felt overcome by a great weariness, as if his body had reached the limits of exhaustion. But the fatigue didn't feel so much physical as psychological. The meeting with his great-grandparents and the high priest Setni, his cousin's illness, and the fear of never getting back to the present had all affected him more deeply than he liked to admit. And the main thing, saving his father, still lay ahead.

Even though he already knew where he was, Sam was pleasantly surprised when he opened his eyes: no more mold on the walls, no rusty machinery, no dead rats in the corners! The feeble glow from the night-light felt like a wonderful source of life, and the ordinary yellow stool struck him as being in perfect taste. He was home!

"Lily, are you okay?" he whispered.

His cousin lay huddled against the stone in a fetal position.

"I can hear you fine, Sam," she said in a thick voice. "No need to repeat everything!"

"I'm not repeating anything, Lily, that's just the echo effect. It happens when you come back to the present. It'll pass, don't worry."

She got to her feet with difficulty and gave him a questioning look. "Are we back for real, Sammy?"

"Yes! This is the basement — our basement!"

Lily put her face in her hands and started to cry. Sam gently wrapped his arms around his cousin to comfort her. Then, when he figured that the effects of the trip had somewhat dissipated, he led her out of the storeroom.

Upstairs, things had been straightened up a little. The armchairs were upright again and some of the books had been reshelved. Leaving his cousin at the threshold, Sam went to the front door, where he saw that a brand-new lock had been installed.

"The grandparents were here," he guessed. "They probably came with the police when they were looking for me. They took care of the basics, anyway. Do you feel up to facing them, Lily?"

"Are you kidding? I can't wait to see them!"

They left the bookstore via the backyard and took a bus home, wondering what fate awaited them. By the clock, their little prehistoric/Roman/North American escapade had lasted an entire twenty-four-hour day in the present, so everyone was likely to be furious at their disappearance. Sam didn't know which he should fear most: the cops investigating the museum burglary or the demonic duo of Evelyn and Rudolf. If those two got their hands on him, they would cheerfully cut him to ribbons and ship the pieces to a juvenile detention center. With the police, at least, regulations forbade that kind of treatment.

Grandpa and Grandma's garage was empty and locked.

"Do you think the Arkeos man could have come after them?" Lily whispered anxiously as she took out her keys.

"I dunno . . ."

They went inside, called for their grandparents without result, then raced upstairs. Someone had certainly been in Sam's room. Clothes were strewn on the bed, the night table drawer stood open, a book bag had been emptied onto Spider-Man's head — the foot-high model of the web-slinger was a gift from his father — and . . .

"My computer!" Sam shouted.

His desk was an indescribable mess — more indescribable than usual, that is — and the CPU of his computer was gone!

"Sam!" yelped Lily from the next room.

Sam rushed to her bedroom. The setting was pink and purple, but the chaos there was similar.

"The loudspeaker!" she moaned. "Setni was right!"

The speaker cover lay on the floor, and neither the Book of Time nor the small black notebook remained inside. The three coins with holes were still taped to the top of the speaker case, however, and Sam put them carefully in his pocket. On a hunch, he went back to his bedroom and saw that his closet had also been visited: The cardboard box where he stored everything related to the stone statue was empty.

"He came, Sam! He came here!"

Just then, the familiar roar of Grandpa's car rose up to them from the driveway, sounding like something between a chain saw and a trumpeting elephant. Sam and Lily rushed outside to greet their grandparents, who gaped at them as if they were ghosts.

"Lily! Sammy!" cried Grandma. "Oh my God!" They ran to her arms, and she burst into tears. "My babies! My little babies!"

Grandpa, on the other hand, was a lot less demonstrative. Wearing his grimmest expression, he gestured for them to go inside. When the door had closed behind them, he exploded.

"Son of a gun, Samuel! Are we going to have to lock you up or what? You just don't ever *think*, do you? Do you know how young your cousin is? What did you get her mixed up with this time? Do you realize that the police searched the house — under my own roof, right in front of my neighbors?"

In seventy-five years, little Donovan Faulkner had lost a lot of his carefree ways. He still made train noises, but now they sounded more like a runaway locomotive.

"Why the police?" Sam asked innocently.

"Because of the museum burglary, smarty-pants! You went there with Harold the other day, didn't you? Well, they found your cell phone in one of the rooms right after the theft!"

"And for that they searched our rooms?"

"Drugs, that's what they were looking for! And then you drag your cousin into it! I'm going to wind up thinking Rudolf is right!"

"Did they take anything?" Sam continued, keeping his cool.

"You want to know if they found your stash, is that it? Don't you have any shame at all?"

"Take it easy, Donovan, it's bad for your blood pressure," Grandma said. Then she turned to Sam. "Yes, they took some papers and your computer. They talked about breaking up a gang of drug dealers. . . . They're wrong, aren't they, Sammy?" she said imploringly.

"Of course they're wrong!"

"So will the young gentleman kindly explain what his telephone was doing in the museum?" asked Grandpa.

Sam looked at his grandparents one after the other. There was no way to back out now. The police were after him, and Aunt Evelyn would happily see him flogged through the streets in chains. But if he was going to save his father, he had to be completely free. Sam needed allies, and who better to protect him than his grandparents?

"Are you prepared to listen to me for at least fifteen minutes without yelling?" he said.

They sat down around the table in the living room, and Sam told them everything — or almost everything. He skipped the most sensitive episodes: the Vikings on Iona, for example, and the Bruges alchemist and his knife, and the bear in the cave. He was also careful not to mention his suspicions about his father's thefts, including the mortgage problem, the Navel of the World, and the Arkeos company. When he reached the final stage of the voyage, the Chicago visit, Sam could feel his grandfather stiffen.

He had no sooner finished than Grandpa pounded his fist on his thigh and shouted, "This is just unbelievable! A bunch of fairy tales! Time travel — is that the best you could come up with? If you think the police are going to fall for even a thousandth part of that nonsense, you've got another think coming!"

"I was there, Grandpa!" said Lily. "Chicago, the Faulkner grocery store — everything Sam says is absolutely true!"

"You've got to be kidding! He was poking around in the attic the other day. He must've come across some old photo albums, and that's the whole story! These are hallucinations, and it sounds to me like they come from taking drugs!"

"Don't tell us you never played with trains in the yard behind the store!" Sam protested.

"All the kids played with trains in those days — in a yard if they had one!"

"You must remember us, then. Lily spent three days up in the guest bedroom! You even came to the train station with us on the last day. There was a Pacific 231, and —"

"The train stations were full of Pacific 231s!"

"Well, what about Zeb?" asked Lily, putting her hand on her grandfather's arm. "Remember Zeb, the little stuffed zebra?"

Grandpa hesitated for a moment.

"Zeb," he repeated in a faraway voice. "Zeb . . . Yes . . . He was black and white, with zigzag stripes. I remember I used to put him on my bed and . . . How do you know about that?"

"Because we were there," Sam assured him.

"So is this . . . is this some sort of dream?" Grandpa was at a loss. "I'm going to wake up, for sure! Nobody can travel through time, right? Least of all you. No, it's impossible." He continued to mutter to himself.

He was quiet for a long time, and they took care not to break the silence. Then he suddenly looked at them differently, as if some veil across his memory had been pulled away. "Sam and Lily, that's right! I'd forgotten their names. I was so little! But the girl was sick. That's right, it's coming back to me. And the boy . . ."

He rubbed his eyes, wiping away the tears that filled them. "You're . . . you're right. There was that business with the two kids at the grocery store. They were bigger than me, and I remember the boy very well, with his knickerbockers and his yellow and orange clothes. I can't remember their faces, though. This is crazy . . . I apologize, Sammy. I never should have doubted you — you or your cousin."

He took both of their hands and kissed them hard.

"You stubborn old mule," said Grandma, who was as moved as he was. "If you'd only trust your heart a little more than your head!"

"To be honest, that year wasn't an easy one," he said by way of explanation. "So many things happened after that!"

"What sorts of things, Grandpa?"

"My father . . . I don't like talking about it, and it took everybody a long time to get over it. But that summer, I mean the summer of 1932, he killed a man."

Lily jumped. "What?"

Grandpa bowed his head. "A gangster threatened him one night when he was closing the store. This dirtbag said to give him money or he and his pals would come after Mom and me. Dad had a gun, and . . ."

His voice fell to a whisper and died away.

"The Browning pistol," guessed Sam. "And the mob!"

"That's right. The investigation didn't turn up anything. But looking back now, with what you've told me, I think I know what must have happened. The gangsters had already threatened him once, he bought a pistol just in case, and when they came back . . ."

Grandma walked over, put her arm around her husband, and finished the story. "His lawyer argued it was self-defense, and James Faulkner was acquitted," she said. "But the poor man was broken, and so was Ketty, of course. Her husband already had a weakness for the bottle, and after that . . ."

Grandpa forced a smile. "When I think that you saw the two of them just before that terrible business . . . At least they seemed happy then, didn't they?"

For her grandfather's benefit, Lily gave a detailed account of their stay at the Faulkner grocery store, stressing Ketty's big heart and James's gruff kindness. This seemed to delight him, and he began to get some of his good humor back.

"I like that a lot better!" he said happily. "And if they helped you seventy-five years ago, it would be pretty sad if your grandmother and I didn't do the same today! Not that I think it's going to be easy. Remember, the police are still looking for Sam, and Evelyn is on the warpath. What do you plan to do?"

"Do you know where Mom is now?" asked Lily, sounding worried.

"Rudolf took her to the doctor to renew her prescription for tranquilizers," said Grandma, sighing. "When she found out that you'd disappeared, she had hysterics. She hasn't been very well these last days, but if we break it to her gently, without rushing her, I think she'll understand. I'll take care of everything."

"No way!" said Sam. "Letting anyone else know about the stone statue is impossible, and especially not Aunt Evelyn! Dad's life depends on it! I have a coin from the right time period and the Chinese capsule to get me there. I absolutely have to try to bring him back without anybody else getting involved."

"You mean to go to that Dracula person?" asked his grandmother, dismayed. "In that medieval castle, with knights everywhere ready to kill you? Sammy, you can't be serious!"

"I can take care of myself, Grandma. Otherwise I wouldn't have made it this far! But I'll tell you what: Before I go, I promise I'll learn everything I can about Vlad Tepes. That way, all the odds will be in my favor. It'll just be a matter of a quick round-trip."

"What if you're taken prisoner there?"

Unexpectedly, Grandpa came to his grandson's rescue. "Martha, do you think Sam could live as a man and look himself in the face if he abandoned his father? I reproached myself for years for not being able to help mine. Besides, Allan sent his call for help to Sammy, didn't he? That shows he trusts him more than anybody else. What more proof you need? If I were younger . . ."

But Grandma wasn't giving up that easily. "What about the police? And Evelyn? What are we going to tell them?"

Lily raised her hand, like at school. "I've got an idea," she said. All eyes turned to her. "I ran away."

"What?"

"Yeah, I ran away. The main problem is that my mom and the police think our disappearances are connected, right? And that somehow it's all Sammy's fault. We just have to separate the two. So we'll say I ran away."

"Mind telling us a little more about that?" asked Grandpa warily.

"Let's say I was really in love with Jennifer's brother Nelson, and I decided to run away to visit him at summer camp. On the way there, I realized what I was doing was stupid, so I turned around and came home. Nothing to do with my dumb cousin!" She grinned at Sam.

"Running away — you?" asked Grandma, astonished.

"I'm twelve years old, it's the right age for that sort of thing," she said firmly. "Besides, it'll be fun to do a little acting."

"And what about Sam in all this?"

"Sam goes into hiding long enough to do his research and get his father. When he brings Uncle Allan home, these disappearances won't seem very important."

"But where can he hide?" asked Grandpa. "Evelyn will be back here soon, and the police could show up at the bookstore any time, especially after the break-in the other evening."

Sam raised his hand in turn.

"Um, I think I have an idea too."

CHAPTER NINETEEN

Vacation Homework

Was this really a good idea? Sam studied the bedroom walls, which were covered with posters for the Blond Satans, an obscure hard-rock group leaning to Goth metal. Its members favored provocative outfits — leather jackets with lace ruffles — and outrageous eye makeup, but had the cherubic faces of kids just out of high school. Sam dropped his book bag on the bedspread, which was decorated with a large skull, and tried to look pleased.

"Cheerful, isn't it?" sighed Helena Todds. "Rick is fascinated by all this morbid stuff. I don't know where it comes from!"

"He'll get over it," Sam assured her. "I've had lots of friends like him."

"I'm glad to hear that — it means this won't seem too weird to you! Anyway, Rick is at his grandmother's for three weeks, so you're welcome to use the room."

Sam silently wished Grandmother Todds good luck, condemned as she was to spend part of her summer listening to the Blond Satans.

"I'll let you settle in," she continued. "Alicia probably won't be back until late this afternoon, but if you need anything, I'll be downstairs. We eat dinner around eight."

Sam thanked Mrs. Todds again and even gave her a hug. As soon as she learned that Sam's father had been missing for two weeks and his relationship with his aunt was getting stormy, Helena had welcomed him with open arms. Sam guessed that she still felt guilty about neglecting him after his mother's death and was eager to make it up to him. What Alicia would think about his arrival, however, remained to be seen.

Sam cleared away the clutter on Rick's desk — funny how irritating another person's mess can be — and set down the stack of books he had checked out of the library: a history of Romania, local maps, a biography of Dracula, and so on. His plan was simple: to lie low for a couple of days, avoiding everybody who was after him, and study up on Vlad Tepes. Didn't people say that to defeat your enemy, you must know him first? The clearer the picture he had of Vlad, and the more he knew about Vlad's habits and his life at the castle, the easier it would be for him to rescue his father.

When Sam had pushed the stack of Gothic magazines and bumper stickers aside ("Eternity Is Gothic," "Doom Metal Is Above Music"), he took out a pen and paper. It was time to get to work.

He quickly discovered that it was difficult to describe Vlad Tepes in a few words, other than the fact that he wasn't the sort of guy you'd invite for a fun weekend. Vlad's father, the *voivode* — or duke — of the Romanian province of Wallachia, was the victim of an unhappy geographical situation: His country lay right where the Christian and Muslim worlds met, at the junction of trade routes linking Europe to Asia. As a result, he spent most of his life waging war before being assassinated by the Hungarians. In the Middle Ages, it was a common practice to force a defeated enemy to leave his sons with the victor, and little Vlad spent his childhood bouncing between Wallachia, Transylvania, and the Turkish sultan's court, where he spent four years as a hostage.

It was a troubled and somewhat sad childhood, but he recovered to seize the throne of Wallachia in a daring coup in 1456, when he was about twenty-eight. The same causes produce the same results, however, and Vlad quickly realized that he was the filet mignon sandwiched between the Turks and the Hungarians. Everybody drooled over Wallachia, and Vlad soon found himself waging war in turn, determined not to be swallowed whole by his ravenous neighbors.

At that point, things started to get weird. To make himself completely inedible, as it were, Vlad imposed a reign of terror on his subjects, mercilessly executing anybody — man, woman, or child — whom he felt might possibly be a threat to him, no matter how remote. Chronicles of the time included bloody accounts of the voivode of Wallachia chopping up relatives, monks, advisers, soldiers, Turks, Hungarians, city dwellers, country dwellers, and every other kind of dweller. Worse, he reveled in torturing people, in ways each more horrible than the next: thieves boiled alive in huge pots, rebels tossed onto enormous bonfires, prisoners given crawfish to eat that had fed on their relatives' brains, and a thousand other such delights.

But Vlad's point of pride, so to speak, was unquestionably

the stake, which earned him the name "Tepes," or "Impaler." He apparently liked nothing better than to see forests of stakes — as many as several thousand, according to some records — on which he'd had his enemies skewered, without distinction of age or sex. Even if these descriptions were somewhat exaggerated, Allan had clearly picked one of the cruelest jailers in history.

Someone knocked on the door, and Alicia entered without waiting for an answer. She was wearing a tennis outfit and looked wonderful, her skin already tan from the June sun and her blond hair pulled back in a neat ponytail, but she was frowning. She glared at Sam, then went to sit on her brother's bed with her knees drawn up under her chin and a sulky expression on her face.

Sam turned to her and stammered, "I'm — I'm sorry, Alicia, I should have asked what you thought about it first. But when I came here two days ago, I had no intention of moving in with you, I swear. It's just that things are pretty bad at home and —"

She gestured to him to be quiet and not pay any attention to her. His cheeks suddenly burning, Sam felt at a loss. He knew he'd acted pretty high-handedly in imposing his presence on her, but at the same time, he couldn't help but think her gorgeous, more beautiful than beautiful, the ethereal Queen of the Elves lost in a dark cavern. And he, the unattractive, miserable human insect, felt thrilled to be there despite the shame he was feeling. Completely pathetic!

Since Alicia remained stubbornly silent, he tried to go back to work. But the words danced on the page, and he felt incapable of reading a single whole sentence. His heart was beating

193

so hard he had to hold his chest to keep it from bursting out. But none of this mattered, because he was so close to her — not six feet away.

Finally, after what felt like half an hour, Alicia decided to speak. "Mom says that your dad has disappeared. Is that true?" Her tone wasn't exactly friendly.

"Yes. We haven't had any word for two weeks. But I promise I'll only be here for a couple of days, just long enough to —"

"That's not what I'm angry about," she interrupted. "Jerry and I had a fight."

"Oh . . . I'm sorry."

"It's not enough to always be sorry, Sam! We had the fight because of you! Jerry told me he was going to call Monk, and the two of them were going to beat you up if you tried to see me again."

Paxton and Monk — like great-grandfathers, like great-grandsons!

"They've had it in for me ever since I beat them in the judo tournament," said Sam cautiously.

"This has nothing to do with judo!" Alicia snapped. "It has to do with me! I had to tell Jerry *again* that there was nothing between us, and I got really angry."

"That was the right thing to do. If he doesn't trust you, he doesn't deserve you."

"I'm not sure he deserves me, but if he runs into you somewhere —"

"I'm not afraid of Jerry, Alicia," said Sam forcefully. "Not on the judo mats and not off them. But if he ever hurt you, he'd have to deal with me."

The words just spilled out without his even thinking, and they happened to be true. Alicia must have appreciated them, because she seemed to relax a little.

She hopped off the bed and came over to look at the books on the desk. "Are you doing schoolwork? Aren't you on vacation?"

"Yeah, but I made a deal with my history teacher. My grades weren't so great this year, so I have to write an extra paper on the Middle Ages. He picked Vlad Tepes — Dracula, that is."

"Dracula? Your history teacher is kind of weird, don't you think?"

Helena Todds called from downstairs just then, saving Sam from having to answer. "Soup's on, kids!"

They spent most of the evening together, listening to music and talking a little. Alicia was still defensive, and she didn't miss a chance to boast of Jerry's boundless good qualities — aside from his obsessive jealousy, of course. But overall, Sam hadn't felt so happy since . . . since when, actually?

The next morning, while Alicia was still asleep, Sam returned to his overview of Dracula's adventures. Like most bloody tyrants, Vlad Tepes came to a bad end. After a cruel six-year reign, he was dethroned by the sultan of Turkey and thrown into prison. But that apparently didn't stop him from indulging in his taste for torture, catching mice and impaling them on little sticks — definitely a creepy guy. A long period of exile and many intrigues followed. Then just when Vlad was about to reconquer Wallachia, one of his own men attacked him from behind and cut off his head. Strangely enough, his former subjects didn't turn out in droves to mourn his passing.

Except that the story didn't end there. Long after his death, Vlad Tepes's dark legend became embroidered with ever more frightening episodes until it merged with the character of the most feared creature in local folklore: the vampire. Vlad was now being called Dracula, which roughly translates as "Son of the Devil," but also referred to his father's membership in the prestigious Order of the Dragon, as *draco* means dragon in Latin. At the end of the nineteenth century, Bram Stoker used these various elements to create the fictional character Dracula, who would take on mythic dimensions and eclipse the actual story of the voivode of Wallachia.

Sam closed the biography and took out one of the coins with holes that his father had left with their neighbor Max before disappearing. A black snake coiled around the hole, which was obviously no accident: snake = dragon = Dracula. Allan had chosen this means to help his son find him, in case things turned out badly. And thanks to this coin and the Chinese empress's magic capsule, Sam would soon be at Bran Castle.

If nothing went wrong, for once.

Around ten a.m., he got a call on the cell phone that Grandma had temporarily lent him. It was Lily, with the good news that Evelyn and Rudolf had come home and were so happy to see her they had bought her story about her running away without batting an eyelash. Evelyn had even been more affectionate than ever, promising to spend more time with her daughter. They had barely mentioned Sam, except to again deplore his lack of manners and moral fiber, the result of the disastrous example set by his father. The same old song and dance, in other words. Lily concluded by announcing that

Grandpa wanted to stop by the Toddses' with a present as soon as he could. What was the present? She didn't know.

Back at his desk, Sam studied the maps of Bran Castle. He was surprised to learn that it wasn't actually in Wallachia but in Transylvania, a little farther north. From what Sam had read so far, nothing proved that Vlad had actually lived at Bran Castle, but his life was so full of unknowns that anything was possible. Nowadays, the castle was billing itself as Dracula's home and had made its reputation among tourists who were fascinated with the character. But it presented Sam with one serious obstacle: The fortress had undergone major architectural changes since Vlad's time, and Sam didn't have the original plans. Entire sections of the structure could have collapsed and been rebuilt, enlarged, or razed. How would he be able to find his way around the castle under those conditions? He had to find a reliable way to orient himself if he wanted to be sure to reach the dungeon.

"Sam! Look what Rick sent me!" In a delicious gust of flowers and cinnamon, Hurricane Alicia burst into the room, waving her cell phone. Sam leaned over the small color screen and saw a badly framed photo of a painting he knew well: the portrait of Yser, painted in Bruges in 1430!

"Apparently you told Mom about it and she asked Grammy to go look in the attic."

"Yeah, I saw a TV program about somebody called Baltus. The painting struck me and —"

"Mom thinks it might be one of our ancestors. Do you think she looks like me?"

Sam angled the phone to reduce the glare. "Yeah, quite a bit."

"Cool, isn't it, having an ancestor who looks like you?"

"I'm sure she was really nice," ventured Sam, who knew exactly what he was talking about.

"When you think this painting was sitting up in an old trunk for fifty years, and that without you . . ."

As Sam studied the image, Alicia noticed the sheet of paper where he had copied the contents of the small black notebook. "What's this?"

"Oh, that? It's another exercise the history teacher gave me. A kind of historical puzzle."

"A puzzle, eh?" She began reading the elements aloud: "Meriweserre equals O . . . Xerxes, 484 B.C. . . . Izmit, around 1400? . . . Your history teacher isn't just strange, he's totally nuts!"

She leaned over and looked Sam full in the face, her blue eyes locked with his. "What are you hiding from me, Sammy?"

He struggled not to look away. "Nothing, Alicia! I'm not hiding anything, I swear."

Her face was barely eight inches from his, and she was so beautiful he could hardly stand it.

"You forget I know you, Sam. After all these years, I can still tell when you're lying. What's going on? Your dad vanishes one day, you move in here because you're not getting along with anybody, you lock yourself away for hours working on Dracula and some crazy puzzle, and then you see a painting on TV that just happens to be in my grandmother's attic!"

"It's a copy," he stammered. "It must be a copy. Artists often used to copy each other."

Alicia nodded slowly, then stroked his cheek affectionately. "Too bad," she murmured. "You don't really trust me either."

She picked up her cell phone and took a step toward the door. "I'm going over to Melissa's this afternoon. We're planning a camping trip."

Sam struggled to get his pounding heart under control. "Will you be gone long?"

"The day after tomorrow. Want to come along?"

An invitation . . . Sam's brain started to boil. Under any other circumstances, he would have loved to go camping with Alicia — he wouldn't have liked anything better in the world! But the day after tomorrow meant two days, and two days here meant two more whole weeks in jail for his father. He just couldn't do it.

"I'm sorry, Alicia," he said dully. "I already have plans."

"Okay, Mr. I'm Sorry. Have fun with your homework!"

She turned on her heel and went out, leaving Sam feeling shattered. *You total idiot!* he raged. Sam Faulkner, the village idiot! Why hadn't he taken the opportunity to talk to her, to admit everything? Maybe she would have understood. Maybe she could even have forgiven him. Maybe they could have . . . *Maybe, maybe, maybe!*

After Alicia left, Sam found himself eating lunch alone, as the Toddses were at work. Then he went back to Rick's room and switched on the computer. This time he planned to use the Internet to do research on Bran Castle. After many false starts — the Net had legions of Dracula nuts, enough to fill several asylums — he began to find information about Transylvania. And link by link, he located a Vlad Tepes discussion group that was about something more than blood-soup recipes and glow-in-the-dark vampire teeth. From an Australian Web surfer he got the URL of a role-playing site that sounded intriguing: Its home page was straight out of Dungeons & Dragons, but the site also had detailed maps of the various castles the voivode had occupied. In that way, Sam found a game called Strigoi Night for which the game master — a Romanian student who knew English — had drawn on his university's archives to re-create the original plans of Bran Castle. Better yet, the young historian claimed there had once existed an underground passage designed to evacuate the castle in case of emergency. This passageway apparently came out in a mill below the fortress and had been sealed up in the eighteenth century because of rockfalls. Sam feverishly wrote all this information down, feeling that he was getting closer to his goal. Vlad Tepes had better watch out!

The afternoon was almost over when Grandpa rang the front doorbell. He looked both relieved and preoccupied, a feat that involved every single wrinkle in his face and made him look like a withered old apple. He was holding a big plastic bag, which he clumsily tried to hide behind his leg.

"It's been a long time since I was here last," he said, sitting down on the living room sofa. "The Toddses are wonderful people, aren't they?"

"They've been really nice to me."

"So much the better. Your grandmother sends her love, Sammy, and so does your cousin."

"Any problems with Evelyn?"

"No. As Lily probably told you, her plan worked perfectly. Evelyn was so happy, she got Rudolf to speak to the police chief and have them give back the things they seized. I left most of it at home, but I thought you'd like to see this." He pulled the Book of Time out of his plastic bag.

"My God!" cried Sam. "What happened to it?"

The big volume's red cover was more battered than usual, scarred with scuff marks and scratches. It was also faded here and there, as if it had been left out in the sun and the weather.

"You'd almost think it had aged in two days," said Sam in astonishment.

"That's not all," added Grandpa. "Lily says that some pages have been torn out."

Nervously Sam opened the book. It was true: A number of pages were missing. Some had been carefully cut, others simply ripped out. The greater part remained, however, and they showed engravings of the town of Sainte-Mary in 1932. Each page bore the same title: "Sainte-Mary Country Fairs."

"Setni was right!" cried Sam. "The Arkeos man did try to keep us from coming back! But what about the police? How do they explain its condition?"

"It's pretty strange," answered Grandpa. "They claim that all the evidence was stored under lock and key and no one had access to it. Anyway, we can deal with the police later. Have you been making any progress?"

"Yes. I got hold of a plan of Bran Castle. That should save me some time."

"That's great. It sounds like you're on the right track. By the way, there's something I want to talk about that I didn't

201

want to bring up in front of your grandmother. Exactly what was your father planning to do there in Wallachia?"

Sam had carefully avoided this topic before, but now he looked his grandfather full in the face. "I think Dad was partly supplying the bookstore with books from the past — and he may have stolen other things as well." Reluctantly he explained the situation with the mortgage and the Navel of the World.

Grandpa scratched his chin. "I was afraid it was something like that. Your father was very worried about money, unfortunately. We helped him out now and again, but he'd become so distant! And that mortgage . . ." He shook his head heavily. "I'm not sure how we'll manage that. Anyway, thank you for your honesty. Not a word to Grandma, of course. You know how proud she is of Allan."

"Don't worry, I'll keep quiet."

"That's good. One more thing: I brought you this."

From his bag, Grandpa took a package tied with string. With trembling fingers, he untied the knot and unwrapped a chamois cloth. It contained a black pistol.

"It's my father's Browning," he explained. "He was found not guilty at the trial, so they gave it back to him afterward. I've never been able to get rid of it. Maybe I was waiting for a moment like this one. Who knows? I've taken care of it, and it's in perfect working order. It's very easy to use. Look here."

He gave a quick demonstration — cylinder, hammer, trigger — that Sam watched somewhat anxiously.

"There are seven bullets left," said Grandpa. "Might be useful, where you're going."

With some trepidation, Sam took the Browning and hefted it, as if to get better acquainted. Should he take the gun to

Bran Castle? he wondered. It was a tremendous responsibility, and a scary one, especially since he'd never used a gun before. But he and his father were facing a man who skewered people for fun. The pistol frightened Sam, but Vlad Tepes frightened him even more.

CHAPTER TWENTY

Bran Castle

Sam had barely set the Chinese capsule on the carved sun when heat vaporized every drop of his blood, as if ten billion needles had exploded under his skin. Then the boiling vapor condensed, and scalding plasma started flowing through his veins. The trip through time had never been so painful.

He lay dazed for nearly a minute, too weak to vomit or even cough. When he came to completely, blood was dribbling from the corner of his mouth, and he had to spit several times to get rid of the bitter taste. *Thanks a lot, Chinese empress!* Maybe Setni would be good enough to check his gadgets' side effects next time.

Sam got to his feet with enormous difficulty, to find himself standing beside a river flowing through a dense forest. The sun barely pierced the gray clouds, and thick foliage blocked its weak rays. The forest understory looked dark and hostile, like the Ent forest in *The Lord of the Rings*. But the tall outline of Bran Castle could be seen rising above the river a mile or so away — success!

Sam retrieved the Browning from the stone's cavity and checked the bullets. It was reassuring to have it with him, though he didn't plan to use it unless it was absolutely necessary. But as he stuck it in his pocket, the huge risk he had taken by not bringing another coin began to dawn on him. He had assumed the wooden capsule and the black snake coin would travel with him through time, so he chose the immediate security of the gun over the escape promised by an extra coin. But the stone statue was empty — half hidden by reeds, holding neither the coin nor the capsule. *He had no way to get home!*

Well, that was too bad, he decided; he would deal with the problem later. First he had to take care of Allan. The best thing to do would be to follow the stream, try not to be spotted, and find the mill. Mills must be close to water, right? After that he could only pray that the Romanian student who drew the castle plans was an ace historian.

After his earlier flameout, the cool breeze felt good on Sam's face as he walked along the riverbank. The grassy path occasionally became so narrow that he was forced to detour through the forest of tall dark pines with scaly bark. The strangest thing was that there wasn't a sound to be heard, not even birdsong. The forest was mute, as if on its guard.

The closer he got, the more formidable the castle looked. It was perched on a rocky promontory, and its two towers, one round and the other square, seemed to challenge the sky. Compared to the way Bran Castle appeared in Sam's time, this medieval version appeared simpler and more massive, with fewer windows and buildings, and less whimsy in the arrangement of the roofs. It was surrounded by a strong wall and looked more like an impregnable fortress than a country resort. By squinting, Sam was able to make out a couple of helmeted soldiers standing watch on the parapet. He gripped the Browning, not fully certain of his invincibility.

The stream led him to a clearing choked by tall grass and dominated by the charred ruins of a stone mill. The water-wheel had been taken apart and its planks scavenged, and the rest of the building wasn't in much better shape. Half of the structure had collapsed, and chunks of blackened beams jutted from the ruins like rotten teeth. The fire must have happened a long time ago, because yellowish lichen had spread over a freestanding section of wall. If the underground passage really did begin there, he would have some excavating to do!

Sam stepped under what remained of the mill's roof and checked to make sure the floor wasn't going to cave in. The place was a tangle of stone blocks, branches, weeds, and spider-webs. The upper floor was gone, and a staircase ended in midair. Behind it, Sam could see a room with arrow-slit windows. This part of the ruin was less chaotic, and some stones had even been stacked on the left. A crack in the floor indicated the presence of a trapdoor. Its surface had been swept clean at some point, and a rusty bolt lay nearby. Someone had gone this way.

Sam looked around for something to lift the trapdoor and noticed a twisted metal bar under an arrow slit. As he picked it up, he saw two letters scratched into the wall: *A.F.* Allan Faulkner — his father had left him a clue! He was on the right trail!

Sam grabbed the makeshift lever and strained to raise the trapdoor, his legs shaking. After two unsuccessful attempts, it finally fell open. The hole below it looked bottomless and as dark as a well. Feeling around, Sam touched the top rung of a ladder about a foot and a half down, so a caving challenge was definitely part of the day's program. Sam wondered if he should close the trapdoor behind himself after he climbed down, but decided against it: Best to leave the way open in case he had to beat a hasty retreat.

He descended a dozen rungs before reaching bottom about fifteen feet down, where the tunnel began. It smelled of moisture and mold, and he couldn't see a thing. He took a deep breath and cautiously started walking, touching the walls as he went. A couple of times his fingers brushed something furry that ran away squeaking, and Sam had to talk himself into not running away as well, in the opposite direction. The passageway finally ended in a wall, and he groped around for a moment before he found a fairly high step on his right. A staircase . . .

The steps were uneven and slippery, so he climbed up on all fours. To keep his focus, he started counting the steps to himself: one, two, three . . . As he reached a hundred and sixty-five, his knee bumped an object that would have clattered noisily down the steps if he hadn't grabbed it. It felt like a fat metal fountain pen with a swivel cap — not medieval material, that was for sure. Could his father have dropped it when he tried to enter Vlad Tepes's lair five or six months earlier? If so, that would mean that this secret stairway wasn't used very much, which was all to the good.

Sam resumed his climb, stopping more and more often to catch his breath. He lost count around the three hundredth step, so he tried to think about pleasant things, such as the first evening he and his father would spend together back in Sainte-Mary. Would they go out for pizza? Bowling? A movie? Or maybe just have a quiet meal at home, a couple of sandwiches in front of the TV? An ordinary slice of life in an ordinary family, that was what Sam wanted!

The top of the stairway was blocked by a low door reinforced with heavy iron straps. Sam ran his fingers over it, but didn't find a handle, lock, or hinges. He shoved it with all his might, but it didn't budge. It was as if it were part of the rock. If only he had a little light! *Come on,* he told himself, *take a deep breath and don't panic.* Resuming his inspection, he found a kind of groove at the edge of the panel. The door didn't swing open front to back, it slid from right to left! And when he pushed sideways he felt it move slightly, even though it seemed to weigh tons.

Inch by inch, Sam managed to open a space wide enough to slip through. Unfortunately, there was another obstacle right behind the door, a heavy wardrobe or large cabinet. He could see faint light on either side of it, and hear a man singing in the distance:

Through the fair greenwood high and low,
Scabbard and tabard, dagger and bow.

By bracing his leg against the wall and pushing with his shoulder, Sam was able to slowly shove the cabinet aside.

Through the fair greenwood high and low,
Stalking the boar, stalking the doe.

Sam was in luck. The man's lusty singing covered the squeaking the cabinet made as he wrestled it out of the way. He squeezed through the space, stretched his leg down, and felt his foot touch the floor. Whew! He'd made it!

He peered around. The stairway ended in an arched room hewn out of the rock: an armory, with halberds, maces, shields, crossbows and their bolts, and small cannons and cannonballs, all carefully hung on the walls or stored on the shelves of cabinets like the one that blocked the underground passage. Sam shoved the cabinet back in place, but left the heavy sliding door open — again to save time in case of a quick exit. The room next to the armory had benches and tables with helmets on them, and a fireplace. The singing came from a soldier who was roasting a haunch of meat. Melting fat sizzled in the flames as he swung into the next verse:

Shadows are length'ning, the moon starts to glow,
Through the fair greenwood high and low.

The singing chef seemed to be alone and completely absorbed in the pleasure of his anticipated feast. But Sam would have to pass right by him to exit the kitchen. The man had his back to Sam and wasn't paying any attention to what might be happening behind him — always a mistake.

Sam fetched a club from the armory — one that looked like a baseball bat with a spike at the end. Silently he crept up behind Wallachia's great singing hopeful.

Home to the castle, the cottage below,
Through the fair greenwood high and low.

Weaving her magic, my winsome Margot,
Through the fair greenwood high and —

The club crashed down on the man's neck with a thud.

"Hello!" said Sam.

The cook collapsed, and Sam grabbed him to keep him from falling into the fireplace. Faithful to the conventions of every infiltration game worthy of the name, Sam dragged him into a dark corner of the armory. Considering the state Margot's boyfriend was now in, it would be a long time before he got home.

Glancing through the guardroom door, Sam saw a spiral staircase connecting the basement and the upper floors, no doubt in the round tower. If he remembered the map correctly, the dungeon was located below the central courtyard, on the east side. The most discreet route was always the safest, so Sam decided it would be best to try going through the basement. He slipped downstairs, where the halls were lit by torches spaced at regular intervals. To his surprise, he didn't see anybody in the basement either. He could just barely hear the sound of marching steps in the distance. Were all the soldiers on vacation?

He began to investigate various hallways, hoping to find the dungeons. At one intersection, Sam thought he had reached his goal, but the barred grillwork he encountered protected only a few rows of barrels. After a few additional detours, he discovered a staircase that descended to the depths of the castle, and this one led to his destination.

He peeked out from behind the staircase wall to get a sense of the layout. The prison consisted of a fairly wide, low-ceilinged hallway with half a dozen cells off it, each with a heavy studded door. A soldier sat on a bench next to a table in the center of the hall, carving a piece of wood with an enormous knife. A pitcher of beer stood within easy reach, and the man was whistling a cheerful tune. Amazing — everyone seemed to be candidates for *Wallachian Idol*!

Unfortunately, the guard was facing the stairs, so once Sam stepped into the light, he would have no chance of remaining unseen. Well, he would need to get the keys from the guard anyway. He took the Browning out of his pocket, summoning his courage to use it if necessary. As he did, he felt the object he had picked up in the underground passage earlier. It was a tear gas cartridge, like the ones his father had bought to protect the bookstore! So it had indeed been Allan who'd used the tunnel from the mill. Had he planned to neutralize Dracula by squirting him with tear gas? Why not use a little garlic spray instead?

Struggling to master his fear, Sam stepped forward, gun in hand.

"I've come to free Allan Faulkner," he blurted.

This sounded like dialogue from a cheesy movie, but the soldier looked up in surprise. He had a reddish three-day beard and a flattened nose with a huge gray wart. "What —"

"Allan Faulkner," Sam repeated. "Where is he?"

The guard recovered. "By my mother-in-law's horns! Who do you think you are, you whiffet? Do you plan to flog me with your little stick?"

If he'd had the time, Sam would have raised at least two objections: He was not a "whiffet," whatever that meant, and his "little stick" represented five hundred years of technological progress. But he was in a hurry, so he shot the pitcher instead.

It exploded in a thousand pieces, and the echo of the gunshot filled the hallway. The terrified soldier leaped back and dropped his knife. "It's . . . it's black magic!"

"That's right," confirmed Sam. "And if you don't do what I say, I swear I'll do the same thing to your foot. Free Allan Faulkner now!"

"Allafaukner?" asked the guard. "I don't know who you're talking about!"

Had his father given them a false name? "He came five or six months ago. Fairly tall, dark hair, blue eyes."

"Oh, the madman! But if I release a prisoner, they'll kill me!"

"Would you rather die right now? What cell is he in?"

The man shot a worried glance toward one of the cell doors. Sam raised his gun slightly.

"All right, all right, I'll open up. But point that strange cannon somewhere else. I don't want it blowing up in my face!"

The guard took the key ring from his belt and unlocked the door. "You can go in," he said, stepping aside.

"You first," said Sam.

CHAPTER TWENTY-ONE

Conversation in a Cell

The soldier with the wart bent down to enter the cell. Sam followed, nudging the Browning's barrel into the man's ribs. The stench was pestilential and the cell's floor was strewn with straw, as if they were keeping wild animals instead of human beings. In the near darkness, all Sam could make out was a thin, huddled shape.

"Dad?"

The figure turned slowly to him, and Sam's heart sank. The man was so thin that his cheekbones seemed about to come through the skin. His nearly closed eyes were vacant, and his hair and beard were so long, he looked like the survivor of a shipwreck. But it was definitely his father.

"Dad?" Sam repeated.

"Sa-Sam?" came a quavering voice.

Sam felt something suddenly snap inside. Big hot tears began to run down his cheeks, and he made no effort to stop them. He cried silently, with joy and sadness, at finding Allan after all this time, after all the ordeals and terrors, at finding him in this pitiable state, but still alive — alive in spite of everything. He cried for his father, for Alicia, and for his grandparents who were so far away he wondered if he would ever see them again. He cried for his mother too, and for the pride she must be feeling as she sat in some little corner of heaven and looked down at him. He had succeeded.

But Sam's relaxing his vigilance for that moment proved fatal. Seeing his sudden vulnerability, the guard jabbed him with his elbow. The pistol went flying through the air, the soldier slammed his muscular body into Sam's chest, and they fell onto the straw. Sam rolled into a ball so as not to be crushed.

"You're going to suffer, whiffet," thundered the guard.

But the yell of rage died in his throat as an unknown figure leaped out of the darkness. Another prisoner! He looped his chained hands around the guard's neck and jerked them back. The soldier reared like an angry stallion, but his attacker held firm. A mix of rattles and gurgles followed, then a long sigh, then nothing.

"What a piece of garbage!" said the unknown prisoner. Then, to Sam: "The keys, quick, before he wakes up. They're hanging on a hook under the table."

Sam first retrieved his Browning, then went to get the keys. Back in the cell, leaving his rescuer to deal with his chains, he carefully put his arms around his father. Allan appeared to have lost half his body weight, and hugging him was like hugging a shriveled old man.

"Dad, it's me, Sam."

"Sam-Sam-Sam-Sam," Allan said in a singsong, his eyes vacant.

Sam saw a bucket with a dipper in the corner. "Here, drink this." He poured some of the water on his father's parched lips.

Allan's body was covered with oozing red sores, and the filthy scraps of a threadbare tunic barely covered his protruding ribs. He was no more than a bag of bones in rags.

"Save me, Sam . . . save me."

"I'm here, Dad. Can you hear me? I've come to save you! We're going home!"

"Sam-Sam-Sam."

The other prisoner knelt beside them to unlock Allan's chains. He was about twenty years old, with a narrow face and a determined expression. He seemed to have suffered much less from captivity than his cellmate.

"You're wasting your time, boy. He's been like this for days. I think he's lost his mind." He stuck out his hand. "My name's Dragomir."

Sam shook it gladly. "Have you been here long?" he asked as he rubbed his father's ankles, which showed the scars of the leg irons. Allan continued to chant "Sam" above his head.

"Three weeks, maybe four. You lose track of time fast in jail. I was carrying pepper and saffron from the Black Sea when my caravan was attacked. The master of Bran is demanding a ransom before he'll return me to my family."

"The master of Bran. Do you mean the voivode of Wallachia?"

Dragomir bared his teeth in what was probably meant to be a smile. "Yes, the Impaler. But you're well informed. I was given to understand that it was quite secret."

"What was secret?"

"The fact that the Impaler bought part of Bran Castle. He's very attached to this place but absolutely doesn't want anyone to know about it."

Sam, who was watching his father, didn't quite follow. "Oh?"

"The Impaler could have taken it by force if he'd wanted to, of course! But a war costs men, and he would have revealed that he coveted the castle. Instead he bought the right of residency to the square tower, so he can come and go as he pleases and nobody is the wiser."

This seemed like odd behavior for a warrior duke. "What's so special about Bran Castle that makes the voivode interested in it?"

The young man avoided the question with a shrug. "If you really want to know, go ask him."

"You mean he's here?"

"As far as I know, he is in Wallachia right now, fighting Sultan Mehmed. The lord of Bran is fighting his own war against one of his vassals."

Sam heaved a huge sigh of relief. So that's why the castle's corridors seemed so deserted! "But if the voivode wants to keep all this confidential, how do you know so much about it?"

Dragomir showed his teeth again. "The notary who drafted the contract between Lord Bran and the voivode was imprisoned here for a few months — to ensure his silence, of course. He died of a fever a few days ago."

So there were no witnesses, and there was no evidence of Vlad. That's why historians found it so hard to prove the connection between Dracula and Bran Castle!

Dragomir jumped to his feet. "We should get out of here. There's not much chance the other guards heard us, but they do make rounds."

Sam put his arm under his father's shoulder to help him to his feet. "All right, Dad, we're going now."

Supported by his son, Allan took a first halting step out of the cell, then a second. When he reached the guard's table, he had to shield his eyes against the candlelight with his hand.

"Where . . . where are we?" he stammered.

"In the Bran Castle dungeon," Sam answered. "But that's all over. We're going home now."

"We're going home," Allan said thoughtfully. "Yes, we're going home!" Then, slowly: "Sam? Sam, is that you?" He stroked Sam's cheek with his fingers, staring at him with feverish eyes. "Sam Faulkner! Allan Faulkner's son!"

"Not so loud, Dad. Someone will hear us!"

But his father didn't care. Mad with joy, he hugged Sam in his thin arms and proclaimed, "He came! My son came! Allan and Elisa Faulkner's son!"

As anxious as he was to get out of there, Sam embraced him in turn. How long had it been since his father had hugged him like this?

"Sam Faulkner!" Allan chanted, at the height of exultation. "Sam-Sam-Sam!"

But Dragomir quickly brought them back to reality. "We can't stay here any longer, it's too dangerous!"

Sam gently freed himself and helped his father to the staircase. Allan was so weak that it took a major effort to get him up the steps.

"Right here," Allan muttered once they were at the top. "Right here, I know."

"What's right here?" asked Sam.

"Vlad Tepes, of course," said Allan, whose mind seemed to be wandering. "He's the one who has it — right here!"

"What does he have?"

"He stole it in Izmit," his father continued. "When he was young. I remember now!"

Dragomir turned around, a finger to his lips.

"We have to be quiet, Dad," whispered Sam. "There are soldiers around, and if they catch us we'll never go home."

Allan stopped dead and glared at him. "I don't want to go home," he said in a determined voice. "I'm not going anywhere!"

"What are you talking about?" cried Sam in exasperation. "Don't you get it? If we stay here, we'll die!"

"I'd rather die than leave without it, do you hear? I'd rather die!"

Sam tried to pull him along, but his father resisted, bracing his legs with newfound determination and vigor. "Meriweserre's bracelet," he muttered urgently, as if that would change Sam's mind. "Meriweserre's bracelet! It's in the highest room of the square tower! We can take it easily!"

"We're not taking anything," said Sam angrily. "I don't care about that stuff! Come on!"

He pulled harder, but Allan let himself fall to the ground and started yelling: "Guards! Guards! I'm escaping!"

Dragomir jumped down and clapped his hand over Allan's mouth. "If you don't shut up right away, old man, I'll make you swallow your tongue!"

"Mmm-ards! Mmm-scaping!" Allan mumbled.

"Tell him to calm down or there's going to be trouble," Dragomir threatened.

Sam was suddenly at a loss. To find his father he had run from Vikings, crossed war zones, faced a bear, fought gangsters, and survived a volcanic eruption, and now Allan himself was preventing his own rescue! He was making such a racket, the soldiers were sure to raise the alarm — either that, or Dragomir would eventually strangle him. What could he do?

"All right, all right!" he said with a sigh. "Dad, listen. If you promise to wait for me by the hidden stairs, I'll go get your bracelet. Do you understand?"

"What hidden stairs?" asked Dragomir, his eyes suddenly alight.

"We came in through a tunnel that ends in a mill outside the castle. There's a passageway in the armory that leads to it." He turned to his father. "You remember that passageway, don't you, Dad? And the big dark staircase?"

With Dragomir's hand still over his mouth, his father nodded.

"Do you swear not to scream?" Sam insisted. "And to stay in the armory till I get there?"

Another nod.

"Let him go, Dragomir. He'll be quiet."

The young man obeyed grudgingly, and they set Allan back on his feet, letting him lean against the wall. They were ready to intervene if he seemed about to yell, but he appeared to be more in control of himself.

"Can you tell me exactly where the bracelet is, Dad?"

"In the highest room, Sam. In the square tower."

"What does it look like?"

"It's Meriweserre's bracelet, the pharaoh of the Hyksos! There's no mistaking it!"

The Hyksos, thought Sam. Setni had also mentioned them — barbarians from the East who had once invaded Egypt. But so what?

"There's just the problem of the cage," Allan added, as if it were a mere detail.

"The cage? What cage?"

"It's valuable, you know. They put it in the cage so it wouldn't be stolen! You just have to open it by . . ." He scratched his head anxiously while staring at the tips of his toes.

"By doing what, Dad?" Sam encouraged him.

"Well, there's a big combination lock on the cage. That's right. And then . . ." He gave his son a look of immense despair. "It's what they've done to my mind, Sam! I can't remember anything anymore! I should've explained things for you better. I feel bad about that. But we can go together, can't we? I need that bracelet, you understand? Otherwise I'd rather die here!"

He was getting agitated again, and Sam feared that Dragomir would step in. He absolutely had to get Allan to the secret stairway. After that . . .

"I told you I'd bring it back, Dad. You trust me, don't you? I got you out of the dungeon, I can make it to the tower."

"Yes, son, of course I trust you! Otherwise you wouldn't be here, would you?" With great gentleness, he leaned awkwardly toward Sam and kissed his cheek. "I've always trusted you, Sam."

"When you're done smooching here," Dragomir interrupted, "I'd really like to take that hidden passageway. And preferably without an army at my heels!"

CHAPTER TWENTY-TWO

Meriweserre's Bracelet

They separated at the first level of the round tower. Dragomir promised he would escort Allan to the armory and stay with him as long as there was no danger.

"But if any soldiers show up," he warned, "I'm not going to wait around. Sorry!"

For his part, Sam took a different hallway, which Dragomir said led directly beneath the square tower. At one point Sam had to duck behind an enormous column bearing the Bran coat of arms to avoid a pair of sentinels coming his way. The two men were joking about a feast planned for that evening to celebrate the return of the lord and his men. Bran was definitely a castle for laid-back good cheer.

Once in the square tower, Sam waited a full minute, listening to the sounds that came to him from the staircase. There were a few creaks, the whistle of wind blowing through an arrow slit, and some distant barking, but that was all. He had decided he would climb to the top room and look at the bracelet and what was around it so he could describe it to his father. Then he would head back down, saying that he hadn't been able to steal it. This would make his father happy and also convince him of his good faith. Besides, any place that had one such treasure could well hold others; he might find a coin with a hole to help them get home.

The tower was indeed deserted, as Dragomir had indicated, and no Bran soldiers were even standing by the doors. Through a crude glass window at the second landing, Sam saw a kind of living room with red curtains on the wall and dark wood chests. As he climbed three more stories, the steps gradually narrowed. At one point, they were little more than toeholds, and the stairway walls pressed in so tightly he could feel the coolness of the rock through his linen shirt. After ten more steps, Sam came to a heavy door bound with iron bands and flanked by two wicked-looking lances with jagged blades. The door's circular handle was in the shape of an undulating snake biting its own tail. Sam hesitated to turn it. After all, if an object as precious as Meriweserre's bracelet was really here, the door would surely be locked. But when he pushed down on the snake, the heavy door swung open.

From the threshold, Sam saw a square chamber that was open on all sides. Wide windows overlooked valley and forest, providing an extraordinary panorama of a sea of tall dark pine trees, some gray rock, the colored roofs of some nearby farm buildings, and the sky, close enough to touch. Under each window stood a black bench, supported by legs carved to resemble those of various animals. The seats were covered in vermilion cloth embroidered with images of armored knights battling lions or griffins. Slender ivory columns stood between the windows, decorated with an astonishing number of tiny grimacing faces. Were they meant to represent Vlad Tepes's victims?

This strange little room was otherwise empty except for a central pedestal that supported a wrought-iron cage. As Sam walked over to examine it, he noticed a portcullis mounted directly above the door. Apparently the chamber was usually protected by the grille; it seemed odd that no one had thought to lower it.

The cage was a cube about twenty inches square, with bars shaped like big, waving flames welded together. Inside was a striking miniature model of the entire high tower chamber, eighteen inches on each side, with the same gray wooden window casements, tiny ivory columns, and finger-length black benches with red cushions. A gold bracelet lay in the center on a silver stand . . . Meriweserre's bracelet, surely. It glowed with an unearthly radiance, almost seeming to give off its own light: a solid gold circle with a small screw clasp, engraved with a series of simple slits — and a tiny little sun with six rays.

Suddenly Sam realized what lay in front of him. Meriweserre's bracelet was the second golden circle! When combined with the seven coins, it was one of only two objects in the world that allowed a person to control his destination in time!

A number of previously random elements suddenly fell into place. Meriweserre, to begin with: the Hyksos pharaoh who had conquered Egypt and looted Imhotep's treasure. Sam remembered the list he had labored over at the end of the black notebook. "Meriweserre = O" must mean that the Hyksos pharaoh was the one who had made the object — a copy of Setni's original — since O could stand for object or the shape of the bracelet itself. After that, the golden circle must have passed through different hands — Xerxes, Caliph Al-Hakim — at different times — 484 B.C., 1010 — and different places — Isfahan, for example — before winding up with Vlad Tepes, its final possessor: "V. = O". From what Allan said a few moments ago, Vlad had stolen it in the city of Izmit. Allan must have set his sights on Bran Castle in the hope of pocketing the million dollars the jewel was certainly worth!

Sam tried to squeeze his fingers between the metal flames, but the cage was designed to thwart anyone reaching inside. "Some have gone mad at the idea of possessing it," said Setni. Had that happened to Allan Faulkner? Sam had to admit there was something fascinating about the bracelet, especially considering its immense powers. How would Vlad Tepes use them, for that matter? And why display this marvel here in the square tower, unguarded?

Sam examined the locking mechanism. The base of the cage was held shut by a four-inch iron jaw operated by the big combination lock his father had warned him about. The lock consisted of four cylinders — each marked with a series of numbers — mounted side by side, with a lever shaped like a wolf's head on the right. You entered the combination, pulled the lever, and got the bracelet — maybe.

He rotated one of the cylinders: 1-2-3-4-5-6-7-8-9-0. That meant there were 10,000 possible solutions. So why didn't the Bran soldiers try their luck? Weren't they gamblers? Or they were afraid of something?

Sam inspected the stand the cage rested on, a column of solidly intertwined crossbars. Inside it, he could see a pulley and the links of a chain that disappeared into the floor. So the lock operated some other mechanism in addition to the one that opened the cage.

Sam walked over to the nearest window, the one that overlooked the castle courtyard, and glanced down. One guard was casually pacing along the parapet; another was sitting on a barrel, jug in hand. Nobody seemed overly concerned about the square tower and its fabulous treasure. But when Sam looked at the top edge of the window frame, he understood why: A portcullis with razor-sharp spikes was hidden in the thickness of the wall. The other windows had them too.

Okay, Sam told himself. *Either the guy who gets here enters the winning combination the first time and bingo! He hits the jackpot. Or the four numbers he enters are wrong, and the grilles all crash down at the same time.* Suddenly the room itself would become a cage, a large-scale replica of the one around Meriweserre's bracelet. Diabolical! And enough to cool the hopes of any Bran soldier, especially considering what would follow: an intimate chat with Dracula!

Sam now knew enough to give his father a convincing picture of the situation. Allan would surely agree that he'd made the only possible decision: not to take a stupid chance. He stood one last time in front of the golden circle, wondering if a million dollars even came close to its real value. The perfection of the jewel's shape, the almost unreal glow it gave off, the striking simplicity of its design — did that actually have a price? To think it would take only four numbers to be able to seize it. Four little numbers — not much at all!

"Some have gone mad at the idea of possessing it," repeated the little voice in Sam's mind, and he shook his head to drive it away. For Allan to have successfully tracked the bracelet to the highest room in Bran Castle, he had to have assembled a colossal amount of information. Ditto to learn about the cage and the lock. Having done that, would he have ventured into Dracula's lair without knowing the right combination? That seemed hard to believe. And Allan had left a fair number of clues for his son. The serpent coin, for example, that he gave to their old neighbor Max. The cry for help scratched onto the wall of his cell. And the black notebook, with all its pages torn out; had Allan forgotten the notebook, or was it an additional clue? Sam was inclined to think it was a clue; otherwise, why leave it in the middle of the history section, where Allan might hope his son would go looking?

Once again, Sam recalled the mysterious list:

MERIWESERRE = O
CALIPH AL-HAKIM, 1010
$1,000,000!
XERXES, 484 B.C.
LET THE BEGINNING SHOW THE WAY
V. = O
IZMIT, AROUND 1400?
ISFAHAN, 1386

Could it involve a code? A code that Sam would be able to crack, but a less informed reader would see as only meaningless gibberish?

Yes, a code — that was the approach to take. A code that would have to yield four numbers. But the list consisted of eight lines and a lot of figures, especially in the dates, and they didn't seem to follow in any clear order. From Meriweserre — a couple of thousand years before Christ — the list jumped to Caliph Al-Hakim in 1010, Xerxes in 484 B.C., and then 1400 and 1386. Allan certainly hadn't stuck to the chronology of people and places. Was that confusion deliberate? Probably, assuming he had hidden a message in the text. So would it be enough to put things in the correct order? No, that produced an equally incomprehensible series of words and numbers.

What about the fifth line, the only one that didn't have proper names, dates, or a huge dollar figure? "Let the beginning show the way." Was it the way to the cage? The way of Time? What beginning? The bracelet clearly began with Meriweserre, but what followed that? Because the list had too many names and numbers, maybe he had to just concentrate on the beginning of each of the eight lines. The beginning — meaning the first letter.

Sam looked around for something to write with. A layer of fine dust lay on the floor of the room, so he bent down and wrote in it:

MC$XLVII

That still didn't make a four-digit number, but something told Sam he was on the right track. First, he replaced the $ sign with D for dollar:

MCDXLVII

That was better. Back in the days before Sam went to live with his grandmother, he often used to watch movies with his dad. At the end of the credits, a series of seemingly random letters appeared. Allan explained that the letters — M, C, L, X, I, etc. — were actually Roman numerals, and that early in

227

the twentieth century, producers started using that notation for the dates of their movies. Because people had trouble understanding dates written that way, it might have been a way to fool audiences and distributors, since the studios could release so-called new comedies or Westerns that were already five or ten years old. Whatever the reason, it became a tradition.

Allan had then given Sam a little class in what each letter meant — M = 1000, D = 500, C = 100, etc. — and how to combine them. The general principle was that you added a letter when it was equal to or greater than the following one. For example: MC = M + C = 1000 + 100 = 1100. You subtracted a letter when it was less than the following one. For example: CM = M − C = 1000 − 100 = 900. Sam quickly worked to remember the other letters: L was 50, X stood for 10, V translated to 5, and I equaled one.

Carefully he scratched in the dust:

$$(M = 1000) + (CD = 500 - 100 = 400) +$$
$$(XL = 50 - 10 = 40) + (VII = 5 + 1 + 1 = 7).$$
$$TOTAL = 1447.$$

Four digits, exactly what was needed for the combination lock!

"What if the combination has been changed since your father arrived?" whispered the little voice. *But what if Vlad Tepes figured out how to use Meriweserre's bracelet?* Sam countered. A bloodthirsty madman rampaging through history would mean that all of humanity's safety was at risk! Besides, couldn't Sam trust his father at least as much as his father had trusted him?

He stood in front of the lock and turned the first cylinder to 1, the second to 4, the third also to 4, and the last one to 7. His hands were damp with sweat, and he could feel his pulse pounding at his temples. If he was wrong — or his father was wrong — the portcullis would come crashing down in a deafening clatter of chains and pulleys. The entire castle would be alerted and nothing could ever save him. But if he had guessed right . . .

He had to try.

Sam gently pushed the wolf's-head lever. It caught briefly, then slid smoothly all the way to the bottom. At first nothing happened, but a second later the iron jaw clicked open. A long creaking followed, and majestically the top of the cage unfolded. Meriweserre's bracelet was his!

Sam reached in, carefully took the bracelet, and set it on his palm. Up close, the jewel was even more beautiful. Beyond its own radiance, it gave off the same comforting warmth as the disks of Re. This was better than a dream, yet it was reality: Sam had the second circle of gold in his hand! He had become Setni's equal!

"Congratulations," said a voice behind him.

CHAPTER TWENTY-THREE

Sam the Magician

Sam spun around and reached into his pocket. But when he recognized the figure standing in the doorway, he immediately changed his mind. He would be dead before he could draw his pistol. In doing research on Vlad Tepes, Sam had seen a number of pictures of the voivode, and there was no mistaking him now: somewhat stocky, with long curly hair, a huge mustache, a strong nose and jutting chin, and catlike green eyes that glittered with evil intelligence. Vlad was wearing a red cap sewn with pearls and a black fur coat over a long red tunic. He also had a crossbow pointed right at Sam.

"So the stranger wasn't completely crazy," Vlad muttered. "He said that someone would come."

Sam clutched the golden circle, forcing himself not to move. He knew immediately that this man would never let him leave the castle alive, no matter what he said or did.

"I didn't expect someone so young," Vlad continued, waving the point of his crossbow. "Practically a child. And dressed like a peasant besides. Unless you are just a lucky little thief."

"I'm his son," said Sam soberly.

"His son, eh? How did you get here?"

Sam thought fast. Telling a believable story would do no good because Vlad wouldn't hesitate for a second to execute him. Sam had to impress the Impaler — or better yet, interest him.

"I travel where I please," he said. "Walls can't stop me."

Vlad might easily have burst out laughing, but instead, he examined Sam more sharply. "That is not the case with your father, apparently. He has been rotting in jail for weeks." His lips tightened. "Who gave you the numbers to open the cage?"

"I know things that others don't," said Sam, his mind racing.

"What sorts of things?"

Sam had read a lot about Vlad Tepes, but he had to hit a bull's-eye with his first shot.

"I know you have a mark on your chest, for example — a secret mark put on the boys of your family, so people know you're legitimate the day you ascend the throne. In your case, it's a dragon."

The voivode paused before answering. "Twenty courtiers of my retinue could have seen that dragon at my coronation. Any of them could have told you about it. Not to mention my women!"

Just the same, Sam felt he had scored a point. "I also know that you stole this bracelet in Izmit," he continued. "In 1447."

That was a gamble, but the voivode must have chosen that date for the combination lock because it had special importance, so why not one connected to the jewel?

"Izmit," Vlad repeated thoughtfully. "Only one person could have spoken to you about Izmit. The very person I expected to see this afternoon: Klugg."

Klugg, the Bruges alchemist! The man who had conducted experiments on the stone statue, hoping it would help him make gold! The man Sam had had to confront in his laboratory before he could return to his own time!

"We met once," Sam admitted. "He is an alchemist."

"Yes, an alchemist. And my father should have slit his throat the first time he granted him an audience! He offered to tutor me and my older brother. I was seven or eight at the time."

Sam did a quick calculation. Dracula was born around 1428 and Sam had landed in Bruges in 1430, so the alchemist would have set off for Romania five or six years after their encounter, probably to continue his research on the stone.

"He said he would teach us Western court manners and Latin," the voivode continued bitterly. "But he wanted only one thing: to visit Bran Castle at his leisure. He treated my brother and me badly, and we never learned all that he promised. But I learned something else. One night, when he had drunk too much Wallachian wine, he told me that the Turks possessed a priceless bracelet that allowed one to move around the world at the speed of lightning. And that by using this bracelet in a secret part of Bran Castle, one could find the treasure of treasures: a stone ring that gives its owner eternal life. He said the bracelet was in one of the sultan's palaces in Izmit."

Dracula was now looking at Sam without really seeing him, as if he was unburdening himself of a story he rarely had occasion to tell. Of course, that also meant that once his account was finished, he would have an additional reason to get rid of Sam.

"In the years that followed," the voivode continued, "Klugg advised my father to befriend the Ottomans. He was hoping to obtain the bracelet, of course. And that's when our troubles began. The Hungarians attacked Wallachia and the sultan betrayed us. I was sent to him as a hostage, and the Hungarians killed my father. All this because of that damned Klugg."

With his free hand, Vlad stroked his mustache, which looked like the tail of a large black cat.

"I lived with the Turks for nearly four years. Refined people, who know how to resort to force when necessary. I learned a great deal, and I took the opportunity to ask about Izmit. To my great surprise, I was assured that the bracelet indeed existed, and that it had magic properties. But nobody could remember what they were, because the jewel had been brought there many centuries before. In 1447, my last year of captivity, I was able to steal the bracelet without the sultan suspecting. Which reminds me." His voice deepened into a purr. "Put it back in its cage."

To Sam, this felt like being forced to cut off one of his fingers, but he had no choice: He carefully set the jewel on its silver stand.

"Perfect. During the ten years I spent trying to reconquer Wallachia, I asked all manner of soothsayers and magicians about the bracelet's powers. None was able to help me. I concluded that only Klugg had the necessary knowledge. After all this time, however, the mad dog had disappeared.

"The day I regained my title of voivode, I resolved to draw him here so I could force him to give me his secrets and kill him. It took me many months to reach an understanding with the lord of Bran, to obtain free use of the square tower and to build this high chamber. I was hoping that Klugg would fall into my trap, but your father came instead."

Vlad's mustache framed a predatory smile that revealed his long teeth.

"A poor fool, that one — grotesque and stubborn. Because he refused to talk, I was tempted to impale him at once. But once dead, he would be of no further use to me. I thought a few months in a dank pit would loosen his tongue. But then the affairs of the kingdom caught up with me, as always! One is always making war or preparing for it, isn't that so? One of the sultan's ambassadors is coming to negotiate some 'back taxes,' or so he claims, and I stopped by on my way to see him. And look what a pretty fledgling has flown into my cage!"

He took a step forward, the crossbow aimed straight at Sam's heart.

"I know death well, my boy. I have caused it hundreds of times, and I have seen it take thousands of men and women. It is a curious spectacle. But though I have studied it closely, I always find it disappointing at the end. I do not want it for myself, do you understand? Never! That is why I must have the ring that will make me eternal. That is why I need Klugg. And if you refuse to tell me where he is hiding, I will start in on your father. I will cut off his ears, then his nose and lips, and feed them to the pigs. Then —"

"I've already freed my father," interrupted Sam.

"Then you are not much smarter than he is," Vlad guffawed. "I assume that Dragomir persuaded you to unchain him as well, right?

"Yes . . ." Sam said slowly.

The Impaler now had tears of laughter in his eyes. "Dragomir is my most trusted adviser, you fool! Did you think you got here thanks to your miserable tricks? The bracelet began to glow this morning, so I knew something was afoot! I reduced the sentries' rounds and Dragomir volunteered to keep an eye on your father in case Klugg tried to approach him. I still don't know how you managed to get into the castle, but I'm sure Dragomir will tell me!"

Dragomir, an imposter! And Sam had sent his father with him to the secret stairway — whose existence Vlad hadn't suspected. *Sam had thrown him into the lions' den!*

"Our young wizard seems to have lost some of his arrogance," the voivode jeered. "You have no choice, you little weasel. Either you tell me where Klugg is, or I'll put a bolt through your chest."

"Klugg went back to Bruges," Sam guessed.

"Then that's too bad for you. Unless you can tell me where to put this bracelet in order to get the immortality ring, I will kill you."

Even though the voivode was about to shoot, Sam had no desire to tell him anything about the stone sculpture, especially since the ring of eternal life sounded like something Klugg had made up. Sam was terrified, but there was one last gambit he could try.

Speaking very distinctly, he said, "If I die now, you'll never know the sultan's intentions."

Vlad raised an eyebrow. "What kind of witchcraft is this?"

"I told you that I knew certain things. In my pocket I have an object that allows me to tell the future. If you promise to let my father and me leave the castle, I'll answer your questions about what the future holds."

"And if I don't keep my word?"

"That's a risk I'll have to take. Besides," he continued, emboldened, "what do you have to fear? I'm at your mercy, and the bracelet is in its cage. You just have to give your word."

"All right, I promise," said Vlad, with a sly glint in his eyes that left little doubt about the value of his promise. "So what do you think the sultan's ambitions are?"

"I need my cylinder. If you will allow me . . ." Very slowly, Sam took the tear gas cartridge from his pocket. He didn't dare pull out the pistol; its musket-like shape would likely arouse the Impaler's suspicions.

"What is this new devilry?"

"It's the object I told you about."

"I warn you: if you try to throw it at me or —"

Vlad had his finger on the crossbow trigger again and could fire the bolt at any instant.

"What is that writing?" he asked nervously.

The label on the metal cylinder read, "LACRYMO. Liquid defense gel, 20% CS (orthochlorobenzylidene)" and below that, "Range 5–10 feet." *Just what I need*, thought Sam jubilantly.

"Those are the incantations that must be recited to enter into communication with the cylinder," he answered. "First, I must take off its cap and —"

"I'm warning you: If you lie to me, I swear I will skin you alive."

Cautiously Sam uncovered the nozzle. Now all he had to do was to gain his listener's trust. He stared deeply at the cylinder and began chanting softly. "Ortho-chloro-benzy-lidene, ortho-chloro-benzy-lidene . . ." It was ridiculous, but surely no worse than "Abracadabra!"

"Well?" asked Vlad urgently, sounding both sarcastic and troubled.

"The cylinder says the sultan is laying a trap for you," said Sam, who remembered the episode from Vlad's biography. "It's traditional for the voivode to go back to the border with the ambassador, isn't it? The Turks will be waiting there to capture you."

"The cur!" the Impaler swore. "An ambush! And what will happen next?"

"That will depend on you. If your own men are stationed nearby —"

"Yes, of course," said Vlad heatedly. "We will swoop down on them before they have time to pray to their god! And does your instrument also know how I can finish the sultan once and for all?"

Sam scrutinized the cartridge in search of inspiration, again monotonously repeating "Ortho-chloro-benzy-lidene." The bottom of the label listed user precautions: "Warning! This paralyzing gas attacks the nerve endings, forcing the eyes to shut involuntarily, causing a burning sensation and rendering coordinated movement impossible. Keep away from children!" What about vampires?

"The cylinder says that by disguising yourself as a Turk, you will be able to slip into the Ottoman camp at night. You speak their language, don't you? You will have no trouble finding their leader's tent, and then —"

Again, this was historically accurate, except that in his daring attack, the Impaler picked the wrong tent and assassinated the vizier instead of the sultan!

"A brilliant idea," admitted Vlad. "Disguise myself and surprise them in the night. Of course!" He paused, then snapped: "But how can your cylinder predict all these things? And how do you understand it?"

"It's a magical object. I can't explain how it works. It speaks to me in a kind of murmur."

"Mmm!" grumbled the voivode, not entirely convinced. "If I managed to rid myself of the sultan, that means I would have no more enemies. My rule would be very long then, would it not? Twenty or thirty years? Forever?"

Just six years, buddy, and not a year more, thought Sam. *But I'm not going to clue you in so easily.*

"Ortho-chloro-benzy-lidene," he recited obediently. "Ortho-chloro-benzy-lidene."

The Impaler was getting excited. "Ask it how far beyond Wallachia I will be able to extend my conquests, while we're at it."

Sam paused suddenly, as if the cylinder was telling him something upsetting.

"Well?" asked Vlad impatiently.

"The cylinder believes that someone around you wants to take over the throne."

"What? Someone around me? Who?"

Sam had never been so glad he'd learned a history lesson! In fact it was the voivode's younger brother, Radu, who took the crown from Vlad in 1462.

"I get the impression it's someone in your family," said Sam hesitantly. "But I can't understand the name. You might want to listen yourself."

He held the cartridge out to the Impaler. In his eagerness to learn the traitor's identity, Vlad leaned forward. The crossbow was now pointing at the floor.

Sam pressed the nozzle hard. *Psssht!* A cloud of colored gas shot out that instantly liquefied and coated the voivode's face with a reddish gel. Vlad jerked backward and the crossbow bolt whizzed through the air, slamming into the floor between Sam's feet. Vlad screamed and clawed at his face. "The devil, the devil! Help me! Soldiers!"

Sam rushed to the cage, snatched the bracelet from its stand, and ran for the door, shielding his eyes against the gas still hanging in the air.

"I'm burning!" screamed Vlad Tepes. He had fallen to the ground and lay writhing. "Soldiers, to the square tower! He has killed me!"

Slamming the heavy door behind him, Sam searched for a way to keep it closed. He snatched one of the lances decorating the doorway and jammed it through the circular handle. That should slow Dracula down a little.

Now to get his father!

CHAPTER TWENTY-FOUR

The Truth About Allan Faulkner

Sam leaped past the bottom step. Where would Dragomir have taken his father? They probably first headed for the armory, as agreed. They would have pushed the cabinet aside, opened the passageway, and . . . What then? The best thing would be if Dragomir had gone ahead to see where the tunnel led, which would give Sam time to warn his father about him. The worst . . .

"He escaped from the square tower!" screamed a guard. "Search everywhere! The dungeons too!"

A patrol was coming, and Sam again ducked behind the column with the Bran coat of arms. He carefully stuffed Meriweserre's bracelet deep in his pocket, followed by the tear gas cartridge, then took out the Browning, his only means of defense. Could he and Allan return to their own time using only the golden circle? There was no other choice. He waited until the patrol headed off toward the kitchens and stepped out from behind the column, pistol in hand.

Suddenly a man armed with a lance stepped through a door hidden by a tapestry. He saw Sam and raised his arm to strike.

Sam automatically lifted his gun in response — aiming for the head, as he usually did in shoot-'em-up video games. But just as his finger tightened around the trigger, he remembered James Faulkner, who had once owned this very gun, and Grandpa's sadness when he spoke about him: "A broken man . . ."

The soldier looked to be about twenty, very blond and a bit baby-faced. At the last moment, Sam moved his wrist slightly and the bullet slammed into a lamp with a crash loud enough to wake the dead. The soldier gave Sam a terrified glance and fled without looking back.

Wiping sweat from his forehead, Sam tucked the gun in his pocket and took the hallway leading to the round tower. Gray stone, waves of dampness, sounds of running feet echoing in every direction . . . Luckily the guardroom was empty. That was hardly surprising; it wasn't the first place you'd look for an escaping prisoner. The fire was still burning in the fireplace, and the meat was still roasting — or being burned to a cinder, in this case.

"Dad?" Sam whispered urgently.

No answer. Had Dragomir taken him back to his cell? Sam silently crept forward. On the armory threshold he suddenly saw something move and jumped aside just as a club slammed into the floor a few inches away.

"Dad?"

Allan stepped out from behind the door. His eyes were wild, and he didn't seem to understand why he was holding the club.

"Dad, it's me, Sam."

"Sa-Sam," he stammered.

"Where's Dragomir?"

With his head, Allan gestured behind him. Dragomir was sprawled full-length in front of the half-open secret passage; Sam was relieved to see he was still breathing. The would-be singing star lay a few yards from him.

"He wasn't a prisoner," his father explained hoarsely. "No, no. He says I'm crazy, but I'm not crazy! I was the prisoner, not him!"

"We have to move the cabinet, Dad. Soldiers will be here any second."

Sam slowly manhandled the cabinet aside, but instead of helping, his father leaned over the guard and talked to him.

"And if you wake up again — *pow!*" he warned with a hysterical cackle.

"Shhh! We've got to get out of here!"

Allan suddenly stopped laughing. "Do you have it?" he asked in a loud voice. "I won't leave without it, you know!"

"Of course I have it! Come on!"

"Show it to me!"

Rather than waste time in talk, Sam took Meriweserre's bracelet out of his pocket and held it under his father's nose. "Here it is! Are you happy now? Come ON!"

The sight of the jewel had a strange, almost hypnotic effect on Allan. He hunched over a little more and fell completely silent. Sam took the opportunity to push him toward the tunnel.

"We need some light," he said. "Wait for me a moment."

He returned to the guardroom and unhooked the first torch he could reach. A detachment of soldiers was climbing up the stairs toward them.

"Maybe Ivan saw something," a voice in the stairway suggested. "He was cooking a haunch of — phew! What's that smoke? Ivan?"

A helmeted head appeared in the doorway, and Sam reacted instantly, grabbing the tear gas cartridge and throwing it into the fireplace. The gas was under pressure; maybe the heat of the fire would work some ortho-chloro-benzy-lidene magic!

"Sound the alarm!" yelled the soldier. "Call the guard!"

Sam jumped into the darkness, hauling his father by the sleeve.

They tumbled into the secret passageway just as the gas cylinder exploded with a loud *Ka-boom!* The walls shook, and Sam slid the heavy door shut in a cloud of foul-smelling dust. Frightened screams could be heard on the other side, but this was no time for pity. Sam hurried down the steps as quickly as he could, half carrying his father. Allan let himself be hustled along, walking mechanically and touching the rock. But half-way down the steps, he seemed to wake from a bad dream.

"Sam? What's — what's going on?"

"We're leaving Bran Castle, Dad. Do you remember Bran Castle?"

"Bran, yes. The secret passageway. Klugg —"

"Klugg? Do you know Klugg?"

"It was Vlad Tepes; he kept repeating that name. But I don't know who Klugg is. You believe me, don't you, Sam?"

"Of course I believe you, Dad."

"'Klugg,' he would say over and over, 'Klugg! Klugg, Klugg, Klugg!' Then he locked me up. I was hungry, I was cold, and they beat me . . . Oh yes, they beat me! I spent a long time there, a very long time! I thought I was going crazy, Sam, I swear. But I'm not crazy, am I?" He started to sob like a little boy.

"It's all over, Dad," Sam said soothingly, even though he felt heartsick. "You'll be able to rest soon." He tried to distract his father. "Tell me, do you know if we can use the bracelet to go home?"

"Meriweserre's bracelet," said Allan, blowing his nose with his fingers. "Ah, yes, the bracelet! We got it, Sam. Did you know that?"

They had just reached the foot of the iron ladder when a noisy horde started down the passageway behind them. From a distance, Sam could hear the clank of weapons, men swearing, and "Kill them! Kill them!" The soldiers had apparently cleared the rubble away from the hidden door, or Dragomir had woken up and told them about the tunnel.

"One foot after the other, Dad, all right? Go at your own pace. I'm right behind you."

They climbed the rungs with great effort and came out inside the abandoned mill. Allan slumped against the wall and groaned with exhaustion, clearly at the end of his strength. Below them, the shouts and sounds of running grew louder. Sam slammed the trapdoor shut and shoved some heavy stones onto it.

"I scratched this sign near the arrow slit for you," gasped his father, pointing to the initials *A. F.* in the rock. "It's all my fault, Sam. I was the one who got you to come here."

"Forget about it, Dad. We're together now."

"No, you don't understand. I deliberately —"

Sam helped him to his feet and Allan gave a yelp of pain.

"My back is a mess," he said with a grimace. "It's my punishment."

"Don't think about that. Come on. Hang in there!"

They left the ruined building with Allan bent almost in two and Sam holding him up by the waist. Rather than follow the river as he had before, they opted for the woods, which offered protection in the gloom.

"I arranged all this," his father continued. "You have to know that, Sam."

"Arranged all what?"

"I wasn't sure, but that was the meaning of the letter. I didn't . . . I didn't want to leave anything to chance, you see. I had to have the bracelet!"

"The letter? What letter?" asked Sam, who was willing to encourage his father's rambling as long as he kept walking.

"The letter from the Turkish ambassador. Kata . . . Kata-something. The one the sultan sent to demand money from Dracula. He wound up impaled too," he added, clearing his throat. "Anyway, Kata-what's-his-name wrote back to the sultan and said that at their first meeting, Tepes was beside himself with rage, because he'd just had something very precious stolen by a boy. A mere boy! He stayed angry for a week. I know, because I saw a copy of the correspondence."

"Do you mean that this boy —"

"I — I couldn't be sure, Sam. I thought I could get into the tower alone and grab the bracelet myself. But in case I failed . . . There was a chance you would be in a better position to succeed than me. Do you understand?"

Sam was stunned.

"You planned the whole thing!" he burst out. "The coin at Max's, the William Faulkner novel — all of it! Not so I could save you if you needed help, but so I would steal the bracelet!"

"I really hoped I would manage it alone," said Allan abashedly. "I really did! It's a very valuable bracelet, Sam."

"I know — a million dollars. You wrote it in the notebook!"

"I was sure if you solved those puzzles, it meant that you could go all the way, you could meet all the challenges! And I was right, wasn't I?"

Sam was speechless with astonishment and rage. His worst fears were all confirmed. His father had *wanted* him to steal Meriweserre's bracelet! He had risked his own life and Sam's for *money*! Was he completely out of his mind?

"Why didn't you tell me before you left? Why did you just take off without letting anyone know, and without even —"

He broke off at a clamor from the direction of the mill. Apparently the stones on the trapdoor hadn't delayed the soldiers for long. And there must be a lot of them, Sam thought, to judge by the glow of torches from the clearing and the shouts he could hear, now joined by an even more dangerous sound: barking.

"Dogs," he groaned. "They're going to send dogs after us."

He started walking faster, practically carrying his father now. The forest was growing darker, but carrying a lighted torch under these conditions was becoming dangerous. He beat it out against a tree and threw it behind them.

How far did they have to go? And where was the stone

exactly? They would have to follow the river or risk missing it. They broke through a tangle of branches and came out at the riverbank. Once out in the open, Sam had the unpleasant fantasy that the dogs were practically on their heels. Then he remembered their next difficulty — no coins!

"Dad, is that bracelet going to get us home?" he asked again.

Allan had been breathing with increasing difficulty since leaving the mill. But he managed to smile as he wheezed, "You still . . . you still need your old dad, don't you? Lesson number one, Sammy: Always bury a coin near the stone statue."

"You're not joking? There really is a coin near the stone?"

"I'm telling you . . . You still have a lot to learn, kiddo!"

The news lent Sam wings. A hundred yards farther on, he recognized the reeds and the tall pine tree with broken branches. "Here's the stone, and it's fine!" he exulted. "Do you remember where you buried the coin?"

Allan gestured vaguely toward the riverbank. Sam made his father sit down, his back against the stone statue, then he started clawing at the ground like a man possessed. The vegetation had clearly grown up in the past six months.

"You're right to be angry at me, Sam," Allan admitted. "I haven't been a very good father to you. Since your mother's death, I know I've been . . . I've been absent. You must have wondered what I was doing instead of taking care of you!"

"Well, I have some idea now," said Sam, trying to keep his tone neutral as he continued to dig. "I heard about the mortgage from the bank and . . . Anyway, all those books and treasures must've been pretty tempting."

"Treasures? What treasures? Do you think I did this for money? You know I don't care about money, don't you?"

Sam poured his anger into his digging. "I went to Delphi, Dad, and I just missed running into you there. The Navel of the World sold for ten million dollars in London! For someone who's not interested in money, that's really not a bad —"

"The Navel of the World?" his father said vehemently. "I've never been to Delphi, Sammy! And I never sold the Navel of the World!"

He sounded sincere, but Sam had no time to think about it. The torches were getting closer and he could now hear the howling of dogs straining to be released to hunt their prey. Then Sam's fingers touched a miraculous metal disk with a hole in it. "I got it!" Quickly wiping the coin on his shirt, he ran over to Allan. "Hang on to me, Dad. We're taking off!"

The stone began to vibrate beneath his hand. Trying to ignore the dogs' ever-closer howls, Sam set the golden circle in the stone's cavity and put the coin on the sun.

"I'm not in very good shape, Sammy," muttered his father, putting an arm around his chest. "I'm not . . . I'm not sure I can survive the trip."

"Don't worry, Dad. It'll be over in a minute."

"No, listen, Sam. If anything happens to me, I want you to know I never stole anything. Not a book, not a treasure, nothing. You have to believe me. That . . . that bracelet isn't like any other, you know. It goes with the stone and . . ."

Sam would have liked to pause then, reassure his father, hug him and tell him everything would be fine; but his fingers were already tingling and Time was about to carry them away.

"I'm sure your mother can be saved with that bracelet," Allan said almost inaudibly. "Do you understand me, Sam? *You can save your mother with that bracelet!*"

To be continued in Book III:

THE GOLDEN CIRCLE

This book was edited by Cheryl Klein and designed by Phil Falco and Elizabeth B. Parisi. The text was set in Adobe Caslon Pro, a typeface designed by William Caslon I in 1734. The display type was set in Charlemagne, designed by Carol Twombly in 2000. The book was printed and bound at R. R. Donnelly in Crawfordsville, Indiana. The production was supervised by Susan Jeffers Casel. The manufacturing was supervised by Jess White.